MW01152917

This is a work of ficti
author. Many characte
published accounts and ....age about the
individuals, events and locales depicted. In order to maintain their
anonymity, in some instances the names of individuals and places
have been changed. Some identifying characteristics and details
may have been changed such as physical properties, occupations and
places of residence. Other names, characters, businesses, places,
events and incidents are either the products of the author's
imagination or used in a fictitious manner. Any resemblance to
actual persons, living or dead, or actual events, is purely
coincidental.

Printed in the United States of America.

This book is dedicated to Sue Bella, my wonderful wife, without whom it would have been impossible to complete; to my wonderful family, Carolyn & Don, Peter and Frankie, for their support; to my grandson, Tommy, who helped "Grandpa" over some rough roads. I wish to acknowledge my editor, collaborator and dear friend, Pam Adams, whose input, time, talents and efforts were invaluable in creating this novel.

PROLOGUE

In the large luxurious upstairs bedroom, Connie is lying in bed while her husband Joe sits in an overstuffed chair, holding his head in his hands. The midwife is in total panic, cursing and praying in Italian.

"Your baby he is dead! He is blue! His head won't come out first!" She is crying uncontrollably now.

Connie screams, "I want to die. God, just let me die!"

"C'mon babe," says Joe, "don't talk like that! The doctor said he'd be here any minute. Maybe the baby's not dead!"

A new 1929 Ford speeds up the driveway, skidding into a hedge, and a short, stocky man carrying a doctor's bag runs to the front door, opens it without knocking and races up the stairs while the startled maid looks on. The doctor is greeted by the midwife holding a towel and screaming in half English and half Italian. She follows the doctor into the bedroom.

"Doctor, its'a no use. *Bambino amorta! Bambino amorta!* Madre she is a gonna die too! It's . . . it's the work of the devil! I go pray for her soul."

Crying, Joe says, "Thank God you're here, Doc. It's our first baby. Please, please help my wife!"

The doctor examines Connie and whispering to Joe says, "Get the bitch out of the house (referring to the Midwife). Fifty-two hours in labor and THEN she calls for help! *Felia ala poutanna.*"

The midwife has a towel to her face as Joe escorts her down the stairs. The doctor is working quickly and positively, talking quietly.

Connie says, "Doctor, where's Joe? I can't see him. I'm worried about him."

"He's fine, Connie . . . we need to concentrate on you and this baby. Come on now, push once more! Push honey, push! Dammit, push harder!! I've almost got him turned . . . ahhh, I got him! . . . c'mon kid, c'mon kid, yell! Yell for your mama, big boy!" The doctor slaps the baby's bottom . . . there's a loud cry and the doctor smiles.

CHAPTER ONE

In January of 1909, The Italian City of *Bari* is swollen with refugees. A massive earthquake the previous December destroyed much of Sicily, particularly in and around Messina. Thousands died in the initial devastation and more perished in the fires that followed. The absence of food and shelter has driven whole families off the island. Ferries daily drop their loads of desperate survivors at the nearest port City – *Bari*. There, exhausted remnants of families seek refuge with friends and relatives; others only pause before taking the longer journey to America. *Bari* is a place to rest, to catch one's breath before moving on.

Established residents of *Bari* assume that Tony came from Sicily with the flood of refugees, though no one knows for sure. He has some money, apparently, and that is not unusual with the newcomers who continue to arrive through the tail of winter. Tony is taller than the average southerner and powerfully built. His eyes and hair are typically dark, though his hair will turn white soon after his fortieth year. He has a thick and elegant moustache and possesses two well-made black suits, one of which he always keeps clean and ready to wear. He feels the need to dress somberly – it suits his state of mind. It is true that he has a small stake of money, but his real wealth lays in the discipline of his mind, the strength of his will, and the knowledge of exactly what he wants from the world – rare qualities in a young man of 28. He sets to work immediately, managing to hustle a small ice delivery business from the owner who wanted to leave for America. The business includes four wagons, five horses, a refrigerated Ice-House and two years rent of a house in which to live. The wagons need repair, the horses have been overworked, and the house is too big for a lone man, but it is a place to start.

Tony takes possession of the Ice-House and moves his belongings into his new home on the same day in March. The spring is just beginning, and it will give him a solid two months in which to prepare for the upcoming summer. He spends several days wandering among the crowded docks and refugee camps, always looking and searching for something or someone. That someone turns out to be a woman from *Bari* in her early thirty's, but with a face and body aged from poverty and hard work. She has two young teenaged sons who have been staying alive through day labor and petty thievery. The woman never volunteered such information, but Tony learned it from her anyway. He has discovered that most people will tell you their troubles if you simply offer a sympathetic ear.

"They are good boys, *Signore*, both of them," she tells him. "It's been difficult for them, but they try always to help their mama." She clutches a wooden rosary in her hand . . . "Ah, they have done what had to be done, poor children, but they would be so grateful for a chance at honest work." She peeps at him from narrowed eyes, and he almost smiles at her. They understand each other perfectly. Her name is Karina.

"*Signora*, make sure your sons are here early tomorrow morning. I wish to speak with both of them." He takes her hand in his and pats it gently, a mock farewell. Tony suspects that the woman's hands are every bit as strong as his own. He turns quickly and strides away from the dock towards his newly rented house. Tony prefers walking to riding a horse. He likes looking people directly in the eyes and feels he can think more clearly on his feet than perched on the back end of a horse. Walking helps him prepare in his mind which routes his ice wagons will take. Within days, he knows every rut and rock on every street in Bari.

As he turns into the walk toward the rented house, Tony thinks to himself: *things may work out very well indeed if the woman's children have half the wits of their mother.* After entering the house, he fixes himself a piece of dry bread and a large chunk of hard yellow cheese. *The woman will have to see to my domestic needs until I have the time to find a suitable wife. The business of the ice wagons must come first.*

Tony sleeps soundly as usual and is up early the next morning. He never seems to require much sleep. He supposes that if he lives to be an old man there will be plenty of time to dream away the hours of life, but for now he prefers to be up and about as much as possible. He toasts a large piece of bread over the coals of last night's fire, and eats with it some of the canned peaches he purchased in town. Several of the local women would gladly share with him their own stock of home-canned fruit, but then he would be expected to return the favor somehow. And since he has no desire to do that at the moment, or even to court one of the local daughters (which he has no intentions of doing ever!), he feels that the choice of a wife is a serious matter and not one to be decided over a can of fruit.

Tony leaves his few dishes in the pantry, fully expecting to return with the woman and her children and the dishes would thus be her affair. He walks quickly towards the docks. As he expected, she is waiting for him, standing calmly with her rosary in hand and her sons behind her. "Good morning, *Signore*," she greets him. "How are you feeling today?" Without waiting for his answer, she turns to introduce her children to him. "*Signore*, this is my oldest son, Pete, and his younger brother, Joe." Tony looks at the two boys and sees that they are big and strong. He likes that.

Not a man to mince words, Tony tells them, "I have a large newly rented house here in *Bari* and an ice business. I need two strong boys like you to help me with the business. In exchange for your service to me, I will provide you and your mama a place to live. Are we in agreement?" He looks at Karina. "Yes, *Signore*, we will get our belongings and go with you," she replies with just the hint of a smile. The boys see that their mama is pleased about this new prospect of work and a home in which to live, and they nod in agreement.

Karina is no beauty. Her face and body are war-torn and aged from hard work, making her appear older than her actual years. But Tony sees a future with the boys and Karina. He can see that her children are loyal to their mother, and Tony values loyalty above all else.

He was born in Naples, part of the Naples Mafia in Italy known as the Camorra and "*La Mano Nera*" ("Black Hand") whose motto is "dead men tell no tales". Notorious, he is considered a "traveler", a man who goes from town to town to hustle and steal. Whatever Tony does, you can rest assured that it is not completely legitimate. The authorities attempt to follow him, but he manages always to stay one step ahead of them. Although kind to his family, Tony is a mean, serious, ruthless man who muscles his way into positions where he gets what he wants. Physically, he is huge (any Italian man over 5 feet 9 inches tall is considered a giant – Italians don't grow taller, they grow wider). He has a handlebar moustache and piercing black eyes. If you say something to Tony, you better know what you are talking about, and if he says something to you, you better listen. People generally do what Tony tells them to do and, if they don't, they sense instinctively that anything can happen to them. You don't mess around with Tony.

In time, the friendship between Tony and Karina turns into something more. Karina is a strong, serious, hard-working woman. Fiercely loyal, she adores Tony and makes herself invaluable to him. He falls in love with her.

....

Tony books passage on a ship to America for Karina and the two boys, telling them that he has arranged for them to be met at the dock.

"Karina, you must write to me as soon as you get there. My *paisano*, Raphael, will meet you and find you a place. Soon I will join you in the city of New York."

Karina really doesn't know much about Tony considering the brief amount of time they have spent together, but the thought of going to America is so compelling that it doesn't matter to her who or what he is. She is happy with whatever Tony wants and whatever decisions he makes. She and her boys are sailing to America to find a new life! And Tony will be joining them as soon as he is able to sell the small ice business.

They all say a quick goodbye. Boarding the ship, *The Liberty*, Karina almost passes out from excitement. The boys carry two burlap bags and a couple of blankets as they help their mama up the ramp. The ship is red and green with black trim and seems enormous to them. They are sent down four levels to the lowest part of the ship. The least expensive tickets are below deck in third class where the peasants and the animals travel together. They are almost knocked over by the smell of the animals and the fumes from the big ship. By nightfall, Karina is not feeling well and is nauseous from the foul odors and the listing and rolling of the ship. Karina and the boys huddle on the floor with their meager blankets in an attempt at sleep.

The second night onboard, someone tries to steal Pete's blanket. He is half asleep, but jumps up and punches and kicks the man. Many fights take place among the steerage passengers in the days to follow. Karina tells the boys, "These goats and pigs are right at home in all this filth!"

On the fifth day, a chicken jumps on Joe. A passenger thinks he stole the chicken and another fight breaks out. Karina spies a man and a woman having sex out in the open and she curses them, "*Poutana, poutana.* No shame! No shame!" Passengers are sick and miserable. They are allowed up on deck for two hours a day with many people vomiting over the ship's railing. The voyage is interminable, but the promise of freedom in the great new land of America awaits them. America! The land of gold and opportunity!

After another week, the Statue of Liberty finally comes into view. They forget the sickness and despair. There is great joy as the ship sails into the harbor at Ellis Island.

Disembarking, all passengers must go through immigration and wait in line to sign papers of entry. They must get physical examinations to prove that they are healthy enough to stay in America. They are put in lines according to their name and country of origin. The names of people are foreign to the immigration agents and they often can't pronounce them so many arrivals find that their names have been changed or shortened (often to the name of the town or city from which they came). The agents write the word "WOP" (Without Official Papers) on many records of poorer Italians who arrive without passports or other means of identification. They are made to wait hours on end and it is often several days before the healthy ones are allowed to finally walk freely on American soil.

Toni's *paisano*, Raphael, searches for many hours before finding

Karina and the boys. There are very few people left waiting on the dock when finally he spots them. After introductions are made, he loads them into the wagon to take them to their new home on Sullivan Street in downtown New York that they are to share with Raphael and his wife. Marguerite is waiting on the stoop in front of the flat as they pull up in the horse-drawn wagon. She welcomes them, saying, "Come in, come in! There is bread and pasta." Karina and the boys cry for joy to be in sitting down to a warm meal in a real house.

....

Having finally sold the ice business in *Bari,* Tony sets sail for America. He isn't travelling third class as he arranged for Karina and the boys to do – he's a first class kinda guy. After arriving in New York, Tony joins Raphael and his family on Sullivan Street.

The downtown streets have ethnic names as a result of people migrating from various places. It is a mixed-up culture with the Irish, Italians and Jews forming their own neighborhoods; all tending to stay with their own kind. The Italian immigrants are the sort of people that find their footing right away. They're clever, they're thieves and they're hustlers. They know the streets – whether in the cities of Italy or in New York City in America. Some Italians are greedy and they prey on their own people. Their philosophy is *"what's mine is mine and I'll take whatever someone else has if I can."* As a result of social conditions and the isolation of the Italian community, extortion becomes a way of life.

Tony starts a small ice business with his savings because this is what he knows. He also gets into other things; anything he can to make a buck. He meets people from the same gangs in Italy. They band together and start their own crew, shaking everybody down in the neighborhood for protection. If somebody doesn't like what they have to pay, Tony is called to straighten them out. He becomes a star in his neighborhood.

Recognized for what he is and who he belonged to in Italy, he is eventually welcomed by the New York Mob, collaborating with guys from different parts of the city. He becomes successful and teaches Pete and Joe what to do, how to do it and to have no fear. He tells them, "If anyone gets in your way, break their head."

....

As young teenagers in America, Pete and Joe are forced to go to school. They know nothing of the American way of life and they speak no English. Since they can't communicate, they have few friends. Because Pete is older than Joe they are in separate classes, so they don't even have the comfort of being together. When kids make fun of them, they get a punch in the mouth. Pete and Joe get in lots of fights. The teacher tells them, "This isn't the way to do things here."

Everything is foreign to them. When a black kid walks into the lunch room one day, Joe runs from the room screaming, "Animal, animal!" (He has never seen a black man before.) Pete says, "What's the matter, Joe?"

"He looks like an animal!"

Because he is older, Pete says, "I've seen them before, its okay Joe." When you come from a poor country where life is hard and all you know is survival, you're lucky if you can get up in the morning and have a piece of bread and cheese. The boys are amazed that in America they can go to a store and get a loaf of bread or a pound of lard.

They try to learn, but they don't do well in school. On the streets in *Bari*, they were clever and thrived, but in school in America, they stutter. Every day they work with Tony, cleaning out ice bins and delivering ice, and eventually they drop out of school.

....

Tony takes to Joe because he's a hard worker, learns quickly and people like him right away. As Joe gets older and learns the ice business, Tony lets him use his horse to make deliveries. Soon Joe has his own ice business with his brother, Pete, helping him.

Joe delivers ice to the wealthier people in the neighborhood, among them the Trali family. John Trali is in the construction business and lives with his wife and daughters in a very fine house. They are nice people, but suspicious of others. Mr. Trali is a known Mob boss. He's a big man with mean eyes. Quiet and soft spoken, he is a man who makes things happen.

When Joe delivers the ice, he often sees a pretty girl of about seventeen. Her black hair and green eyes make him drop the ice and stare, but not too long because the family is always watching. Sometimes Mr. Trali smiles at Joe and says hello. One day, he is in the kitchen when Joe is bringing in the ice. "Hey, Joe, sit down and have some pizza that Connie made." Joe nervously sits down at the kitchen table and Connie brings him the pizza. Joe puts his head down and is afraid to look her in the eyes with her poppa sitting next to him.

Mr. Trali says, "Joe, would you like a glass of wine?"

"No, no thanks, Mr. Trali."

"I think you like my daughter, Joe. I like you. You have a kind and handsome face. If you wanna take Connie to the movies, I think I can trust you." At that, Connie turns red and runs from the room. "Go ahead and ask her, Joe, I know she likes you. She is always around when you bring in the ice. But most important, I like you."

If Mr. Trali likes Joe then the whole family likes Joe and a three year courtship begins. After the third year, Poppa John finally asks Joe if he's going to marry his daughter.

"Hey Joe, when you gonna marry my daughter? Have you asked Connie if she wants to marry you, Joe?"

"No, Poppa John, I'm scared she will say no."

Poppa yells, "Connie, c'mere. Joe wants to say somethin'."

Connie enters and Joe nervously stands on one foot and then the other, not knowing what to say. "C'mon Joe, tell her now," says Poppa.

"Uh . . . uh, Connie, I was talkin' to your dad…"

"Geez, Joe . . . Connie, he wants to marry you!" interrupts Poppa John. Connie's face is beet red and Poppa continues, "Okay, that's settled then. Connie, come hug your man and tell him you love him and wanna marry him."

"Poppa, this is the first man you have liked for me. I love him, Poppa." She turns to Joe and says, "Yes, Joe, I'll marry you." Poppa says, "You are the first of my daughters to marry a guy I like. Of course, you will live next door, eh Joe?"

"That's okay with me, Poppa," says Joe.

…………………………..

Papa Trali wants to make Joe successful because he is now married to his daughter and, who knows, they might have a baby soon. He tells Joe, "You're a young guy, you married my daughter, and here's what I'm gonna do. I'm gonna help you with the ice business. I'm gonna get you a couple more horses and a bigger ice station and this way you can grow the business. I'll

Bayside Sand & Gravel Company is on Alley Pond Road in *Bayside* on Long Island. In a small office building that sits in front of a huge mountain of white sand, rock crushers, numerous pieces of construction equipment and 28 trucks, mostly dumpsters, are lined up to the left of the sand bank. The trucks are white with royal blue lettering on the doors: "*Bayside Sand & Gravel*" in very small print and underneath, "*Joe Basilio, Owner*".

Joe is sitting behind his desk. He is 32 year old, good-looking with rugged features, an olive complexion and intense green eyes peering out from thick brown lashes and brows. He is of average height and stocky build, and has the kind of face you want to hug. His great sense of humor, sincerity and humility connect immediately when you meet him. Joe is a kind and generous man and everyone loves him. A self-made millionaire, he has worked very hard for his wealth, although he is always telling anyone who will listen, "*My family is my real treasure*". Usually impeccably groomed, today his dark brown hair is disheveled and his starched white shirt belies the fact that he has been up all night agonizing over his financial woes. Normally very happy, today he is wearing a bleak expression.

The days' newspaper headlines tell of "*the worst stock crash the country has ever seen ... the day of the millionaire slaughter ... 3,259,800 shares sold for a combined loss of over 2 billion dollars in just 30 minutes*". . . "My God, I can't believe this," says Joe, "all the poor bastards." He shakes his head in disbelief and looks up to see his brother, Pete, coming in with Frankie who everybody in the family calls "Sonny". Frankie is Joe's 10 year old son, his oldest child. He looks just like his dad. They enter the office and Frankie goes to his father and puts his arm on his shoulder. Joe embraces his son, "This is what really matters, Sonny - family."

Joe's brother, Pete, is a rough-looking guy with Popeye arms, black hair and a moustache. He always looks like he's mad and ready for a fight. He adores his younger brother, Joe.

"Any news," Pete asks. "Did anything break?" He glances at the headlines.

"Yeah somethin' broke all right," says Joe. . . "us, we're broke . . . take a ride with me, Pete. I gotta go down to see Jack Kaiser at National Bank."

"What about Sonny?" says Pete, "I told Connie I'd watch him."

"He comes with us," says Joe. "Right, Sonny boy?" He gives Frankie a few knobs on the head. "May as well learn how things are."

They all hop in Uncle Pete's pick-up truck and drive away.

....

At National Bank, the bank manager, Jack Kaiser, is talking to Milton Bloomberg, President of the Bank. Milton Bloomberg is a fat Jewish man with a mop of curly brown hair. "It's a matter of survival, Jack, and I'm surviving with as much as I can get." Seeing Joe and Pete enter the bank, he says to Jack, "You handle those Wops."

Jack Kaiser is a tall, skinny, nervous type, losing his hair already. He walks over to greet Joe, Uncle Pete and Frankie. "Hey Joe, it's a pleasure to see you. Hello Pete...and you, you must be Frankie, hello young man." He shakes hands with everybody and then speaks to Joe. "Joe, maybe my secretary could show Frankie around while we talk?"

"No thanks, Jack, Frankie's a big boy now, he can stay."

"Joe, you don't know how sorry it makes me to have to tell you this, but the bank has to foreclose on everything you have. You gotta turn over the heavy equipment and all the trucks...dammit, Joe, I wish I could do something! Damn Bloomberg! Damn Wall Street! You heard that Wall Street just fell apart and died? . . . I guess you heard about Leo? He sat in his car in the garage, closed the door and left the motor on. Lost his produce business, his wife flew the coop. It was all too much for him."

"I know, Jack, but there ain't gonna be no gas pipe for me. I got a wife and two kids and another one on the way. I'll get along. Hell, I was born in Italy's slums. I came over third class with the cattle and the pigs. I'm a survivor."

"I've tried to get extensions for you, Joe. Bloomberg is cold as ice. Banks are closing too, you know? Everybody's losing everything. Nobody is escaping it seems . . . except Bloomberg. He's a greedy bastard."

"Hey Joe, is Bloomberg the same guy that owns the lumber yard?" asks Pete. Joe nods "yes" and continues talking to Jack.

"I know it's not your fault, Jack, but what about my house? How do I get it back?"

Uncle Pete gets up from his chair and begins pacing back and forth. Jack, ignoring Pete says, "Well Joe, when we foreclose, we have an auction." . . . he pauses . . . "Let me see if your house is on the auction list. It should be." He pulls a paper from his desk and looks it over. "I don't see your house listed. That's strange. Maybe it's just an oversight." Jack stands to say goodbye. "Let me call you back tomorrow, Joe. I'll do some more checking meantime."

Fighting back emotion and unable to speak for a moment, Joe gets up and shakes hands with his friend. He manages to speak after another pause. "Thank you for everything, Jack. I really appreciate all you tried to do for me."

"I'll get back to you, Joe. Again I'm sorry. . ." He shakes hands with Joe, Pete and Frankie and escorts them to the front door of the bank. Inside the truck going home, Frankie squeezes his father's hand really tight, trying to make him feel better. "It's okay, Dad. It's okay. We'll get another house. I can help . . . but why does Mr. Bloomberg want our house? Doesn't he have a house?"

Joe tells his son, "Sonny, don't worry about it. We'll be okay." "You bet we'll be okay, Sonny," says Uncle Pete. Looking at Joe, he says, "I've got some money, Joe. Maybe we can buy the house back?"

Joe shakes his head, moved by his brother's generosity. "Thanks Pete, but right now you better get us home. Connie's probably worried sick."

Pete's pick-up truck rambles up the long driveway to the Basilio Estate which is surrounded by lush green trees and high hedges. The property sits on more than two city blocks with tennis courts and a victory garden in the rear. The big front house is two stories high with a brick and stone exterior and an impressive, polished mahogany double front door. Connie, Joe, Frankie and his little brother, Joey, live in the front house and Grandpa Tony, Gramma Karina and Uncle Pete live in the big second house. The truck stops near Connie's new Cadillac and the three of them get out. Joe tells Pete, "Don't say anything to mom and pop and especially not to Connie. After dinner I'll tell them the whole story, okay?"

"Okay," says Pete. "Sonny, did you hear your father?" "Yeah," says Frankie, "but it makes me mad!"

Inside the house, Connie comes in from the kitchen. She is a small, dark-haired woman, very attractive with a curvaceous figure. She hugs Joe. "The gang is here, but you're an hour late. I was worried! . . . The lasagna will be better though, now that it's had time to settle . . . Joe, Papa was saying that the world is falling apart. Are we in trouble?"

Gramma Karina is a typical Italian lady (5 feet anyway you look at her). She is tough but gentle. She has grey hair and brown eyes, a tiny mole on her cheek and olive skin without so much as a wrinkle on her kind face. She interrupts Connie, "C'mon and sit and pray so we can eat."

Grandpa Tony is a large moustached man, the kind of man you feel safe with. He is treated with great respect by everyone in the family. He adores his step-sons, Pete and Joe, but his greatest love is his oldest grandson Frankie and he keeps a strong hand on Frankie when it comes to manners and respect for older people. He teaches him to speak Italian, telling him, *"Sonny, remember you live in America but never forget that you're Italian."* . . . Grandpa asks, "Joe, what happens to our business?"

"Let's eat and we'll talk later, Pop. Pass the wine and the antipasto." The table is full of great Italian food. Gramma Basilio is cutting a loaf of hot Italian bread.

"Mama, you don't understand," says Connie. "We've got friends who killed themselves 'cause they went broke. My poor Joe, he worked so hard to get where he is. Pete would drive that Bulldog Mack sometimes 16 hours a day to get the job done. Joe don't have to tell me. I can read. I hear the radio. We'll be flat broke!" She starts to cry.

"Mama, don't cry," says Frankie. "I'll get a job." Little Joey, who's a few years younger than Frankie, adds, "me too. I can work!"

"Connie, stop it," says Joe. "Let's eat now. We'll talk later. We have much to thank God for. Just look what we have on this table."

....

The next day at *Bayside Sand & Gravel*, it's 9:00 AM and Joe and Pete are having coffee and donuts in Joe's office.

"Pete, we better get the crew to finish the Corona site so we can get paid."

The phone rings and Joe answers it. "Hello" . . . he pauses . . . "Yeah, Jack, I'm fine. What did you find out?" . . . a long pause . . . "Jack, am I hearing you right? You mean Bloomberg bought my house from the bank before the auction? You're saying he bought my house already? Can he do that? That sonovabitch, can he do that!?" . . . another pause . . . "Well, I know he's the damn President of the Bank, but he sure ain't got no heart, does he Jack?" . . . another pause . . . "Well, I have no recourse then, do I? There's nothing I can do. But thank you, thanks for all your trouble. Take care, Jack." Joe slams down the phone, completely dejected.

"*Madone*, Joe! You look white as a ghost. What did Jack say? C'mon, sit down and let me get you some water." Pete goes to the bathroom and comes back with a glass of water. Joe takes a few sips and says, "The bank President, Bloomberg, bought our house with probably NO money. It's funny. Everybody blames the Italians for all the crime and this Jew bastard wins with the stroke of a pen."

"Joey, that's what you think! I'll break his fuckin' head and burn his lumber yard. He's a no-good bastard! He deserves what I give him." "Calm down, Pete. We'll find a way to get our house back."

"Joe, you think I care if they put me in jail? As long as I get this bum, that's all that matters. I stopped bein' afraid when I was 10 years old."

"Now take it easy, Pete. I don't want you in trouble. We got enough right now, okay? Jack wants all the papers on the loans and the inventory turned in. Gotta bring the registrations for all the vehicles in by Monday next week . . . And Pete, that money you offered me . . . we're gonna need it to find a place to live."

....

Everyone seems to think Grandpa Tony had a heart attack, but no one knows for sure. For all anyone knows, he could have been poisoned. He never really retired - was always hustling. Frankie thinks he's Superman – immortal.

They take Grandpa Tony to the undertaker and Gramma says, "No, no, I don't want my Tony here, I want him in my house," so they put him in an open coffin on top of a huge table in Gramma Karina's dining room.

Frankie says, "Grandpa, wake up, c'mon Grandpa, wake up!" He touches his face - it's cold and clammy and feels like wax. But Grandpa never moves and his eyes stay closed even when Frankie grabs his moustache and pulls on it, saying over and over, "Grandpa, wake up!" Gramma finally runs over and says, "Sonny, your Grandpa, he is in heaven."

"No, no, he's right here, Gramma. He's right here, he's not in heaven."

"Okay Sonny, he's right here, but he's also in heaven."

"No Gramma, he's right here. Look." Frankie pats his Grandfather's face and again he doesn't move. They have to pull him away . . . he loves his Grandpa who has taught him so much.

CHAPTER THREE

Forced to move from the affluent community of *Bayside* on Long Island to the poor working class neighborhood of *Corona* in Queens, the family is trying desperately to adapt to their new life. Connie's father, John Trali, has had a stroke and died. Petey, the third son, has been born. Joe and Uncle Pete try to hire on for work at *Bayside Sand and Gravel Co.,* the same company that they used to own. They stand in bread lines with many other men down on their luck. Frankie is now a young teenager in a rough neighborhood.

....

Packing boxes are everywhere. Connie and Gramma are wrapping silverware and candelabras. A big moving truck is parked in the driveway and two men are loading it up. It's a short drive to *Corona* from *Bayside*, but feels like another world away.

Their new home is on the second floor above a grocery store on a rundown street in a beat-up neighborhood. Kids with torn sneakers and patched-up pants are sitting on the curb playing "even or odd" – flipping baseball cards. Other kids are sitting on the roof of some guy's car.

The Basilio apartment is a four room flat with a small ice box and a radiator for heating. The rent is $18 a month. There are plastic curtains on the windows and an oil cloth on the kitchen table. A window box at the kitchen window holds whatever doesn't fit into the ice box in the winter. Tonight, the window box is empty. Joe and Pete are just coming in from a long day and are greeted by Connie, Gramma, Joey and little Petey.

Joe tells Connie, "No luck, honey . . . where's Frankie? Tell him we gotta go out tonight."

"You sit down and eat. You're driving yourself too hard. We got flour and I made pasta and beans with garlic and oil. Delicious!"

Uncle Pete goes to the table and sits quietly with his arms folded. His face is a cold, blank stare. Joe joins him and the family sits down at the table. Frankie enters and goes straight to his dad.

"Hey Dad, I'm glad you're home." He gives everybody a hug.

"Hi, Son. We gotta go pick-up cardboard tonight, okay Sonny?"

Frankie, saddened, says, "Okay, but can't we eat, Dad? Aren't you hungry? It smells so good, Mom! . . .

34

and I hate to pick-up cardboard! I hate it! I wish we were still rich." Everyone exchanges looks.

Connie says, "Don't worry, Sonny. You and Joey go to school and learn then someday you'll be rich again."

"Babe, he's rich now. He's got all of us," says Joe.

Suddenly they hear some kid yelling from the street below. "Hey, Frankie! Frankie, come by the window! C'mon down. I'm gonna break your ass. You know what you done!"

Connie jumps up from her chair and starts towards the window. Joe grabs her. "Connie, stop, don't go by the window. Sonny's got to handle this himself. This isn't *Bayside* and my kid ain't no sissy. I taught him how to use his hands."

"Dad, I'm not afraid of Orlando. He's mad 'cause I took his seat in English class." Frankie runs to the window and yells, "Hey dirty neck, I'll be right down so don't run away."

Gramma's got her rosary beads in her hand and says, "Sonny, I pray to St. Mary for you. If that sonovabitch hurts you, I kill him myself!"

Frankie runs down the stairs and appears below in front of the store. The whole family has their heads out the window. The street is full of kids making a circle. Orlando is a strong looking kid with a jet black mass of hair. He looks like he just came from the garbage dump.

"Hey Frankie, where's your fancy clothes?" Frankie's piercing green eyes stare right at Orlando as he walks up to him. Orlando throws a roundhouse punch and misses. Frankie is a southpaw and a boxer, not a street fighter like Orlando. He sidesteps and connects a left hook to Orlando's eye. Again Orlando swings. Frankie blocks the punch. A strong left jab puts a red spot on Orlando's eye. Kids are yelling, "Hit him! Kick him!" Orlando jumps on Frankie and wrestles him to the ground. He bites Frankie's ear and blood comes pouring out. The kids love it! Frankie tries to get up, but Orlando knees him in the balls. Frankie, who is down, gets kicked in the face. He is bleeding, but manages to get up.

"You fuck, you kicked me when I was down!" He pushes Orlando away. Frankie is full of blood. He hits Orlando three times in the ribs and Orlando falls to his knees. Frankie aims and kicks him in the eye and the face. Two men grab them and break it up. The fight is over. . .

Back upstairs in the apartment, the family sits back down to dinner. Gramma says a quiet grace and passes the food. "What's the matter, Pete? You look mad all the time."

"I'm just thinkin' . . . I'm gonna get our family straightened out. There's a fish store on Corona Avenue. It's closed, but it's got all the fixtures and tanks in there. I found out who owns it and its some guy from Flushing. I'm goin' over to his house and get the keys, one way or another. I'll pay him when we get the money or I'll break his head if I have to."

Connie says, "Pete, don't hurt the man. He has his own troubles I bet."

"It's a good idea, Pete", says Gramma. "In *Bari,* we were all fishermen. But talk nice to him, Son. Make a deal."

Joe shakes his head at his brother and changes the subject. . .

"Honey, this is so good! How do you make somethin' from nothin'?"

The family is quiet, finishing their food. Joe excuses himself, gets up, kisses his wife and mother and younger sons, and says to Frankie: "C'mon, let's go son."

Frankie has cleaned himself up and washed the blood off. He leaves with his Father to go pick-up cardboard. Connie is left with Gramma, Uncle Pete and the younger boys at the table.

"Pete, don't say nothin' to Joe, but the last thing I got is my diamond ring. It's not doin' me any good. Take it to Uncle Ben's Hock Shop, get the money and buy the fish." Pete looks at Connie in disbelief then takes the ring.

"Okay, kid, I will. You're some standup girl, Connie!" Pete gets his hat and leaves.

Gramma exclaims, "Mother of God, what next? I gotta go to church. This is all too much!" Gramma gets her shawl and leaves for church.

After getting the boys to bed, Connie is left alone in the kitchen with the dishes and her "take out" work. She starts putting the Bobbie pins onto the cards that she pulls out of a big brown paper bag. She gets up to make a cup of tea and there's a knock at the door.

"Dammit, who could that be but another damn bill collector!"

She goes to the door, opens it with a gasp and turns white. Peppers is standing there, a man she knew briefly before Joe. He is oddly handsome in spite of a large nose and a too high forehead. He has a black moustache and dark evil eyes.

"Hey baby, is Joe around? He's a friend, ya know? Hey Joe, are you there?" he yells. He pushes his way into the small apartment and sees that Connie is alone. He grabs her, pulls her into him and forces his mouth down on hers. Connie fights him off.

"Peppers, you bastard, you're drunk! Get your filthy hands off me. How dare you come here like this. You're crazy! Joe will be back any second. Damn you, Peppers!" Connie struggles with him and manages to break loose. She gets to the kitchen where she grabs a butcher knife and points it straight at Peppers heart.

"Oh, look at you, sweetheart . . . a real bitch. All these years, never could forget you. C'mon Connie, put it down. You wouldn't stick me, would ya?"

He staggers towards her, but Connie keeps the knife steady, pointing it directly at his heart. Peppers suddenly realizes the danger he's in and stops dead in his tracks, sobering up real quick.

"Know something once and for all, you bastard. There was never nothin' between us. We were a mistake, you and me . . . a one-time stupid mistake. Leave me alone. Go back to your whore and leave me alone, understand? Joe is my whole life, rich or poor, he's my whole life."

"Nah, that's bullshit. You chose him over me for the dough, Connie. It was the dough."

"Think what you want, you crazy bastard! Just get out . . . get out now! I mean it!" With the knife still pointed at his chest, she makes him move toward the door and, as he backs out the door, he says, "Welcome to the neighborhood, Connie . . . you really would stick me, huh?"

Connie slams the door behind him and locks it.

....

Joe is driving with Frankie down 108th Street in an old beat up international pick-up truck. "Hey dad, look on the corner, lots of cardboard boxes." Joe pulls over, inspects the boxes and starts putting them into a large bin.

"Sonny, we can get thirty cents for every hundred pounds of cardboard. Florists always have lots of big cardboard boxes so they can throw dead flowers away."

Frankie hates having to go out in the bitter cold each night with his dad to pick-up cardboard, but every dime counts, and anyway that's how he learned to throw punches – punching the boxes and breaking the seals that keep the cardboard boxes together. He steps on them, flattens them out and after he has thirty or forty boxes, he ties a rope around the bundle real tight and throws it in the back of the truck.

Frankie is busy emptying a large box when he screams, "ayeeeeee!"

"What's the matter, Son? Why are you yelling like that?"

"Dad, I just grabbed a dead animal! I couldn't see it in the dark and it felt funny – all furry."

"Boy, you're sure a brave kid!" They both start to laugh.

Frankie says, "Here's some rope. Let's smash the cardboard and tie it up. We did real good, eh Dad?"

"Yeah son, we did real good."

They continue going down 108th Street, looking for more locations.

As they approach 51st Avenue, they see that *Steve's Plumbing Company* has two large bags of broken iron pipe and brass fittings and a busted cast-iron stove sitting in the alley. Joe says, "Frankie, we're gonna get real lucky! We can get three to four cents a pound for brass, two cents for copper and flatiron. Jump up on the truck and stack the metal on one side then we can go home. Tomorrow is a school day, big guy."

After the iron is loaded, it is early morning and both of them get back into the truck and start driving home. "Dad, look! There's a 'Bungalo Bar' Ice Cream Man! Can I have one? Please, Dad, can I have one?"

"Son, all I got is twenty cents for two gallons of gas. We're on empty."

He hits the steering wheel with tears in his eyes. Frankie looks the other way out the window. "It's okay, Dad, maybe tomorrow."

....

It's 7:00 AM and Connie is making breakfast in the kitchen and yelling, "Frankie, hurry up . . . and be sure to wash behind your ears! Wear your white dress shirt, you hear?"

"Mom, I want the bread hot with lots of oregano and oil on it. My friend Corky will be here in a minute and I'll finish my homework before school." I put on my white dress shirt like Mom said and my faithful sneakers with the hole in the bottom and I'm thinkin' that I'll go to school and probably fall asleep from bein' out pickin' up cardboard so late with Dad or probably get in an argument and get sent home.

We're all pretty unhappy here, but that's how it is. We struggle and work, but my father gets up with a happy whistle every morning in spite of everything. He says, *What's the matter with you guys? C'mon, get up, I'll make coffee.* So Mom gets up and they make a big pot of coffee and Gramma makes a loaf of Italian bread. She puts a whole gob of butter on it and puts it in the oven. I cut the bread off in chunks and dip it in the coffee and there are thousands of these little rings that form on top of the coffee from the butter. I kiss my mom and leave for school. And maybe I play hooky for the day and meet Corky and we go somewhere – go to a movie or go ride the train. We can ride from Battery Park to Brooklyn and spend the whole day on the train for a nickel.

At night when we all come home, Mom makes big pots of *pasta e fagiole or pasta e lenticchie* and soup or macaroni – no meat – and bread. A big loaf of bread costs eight cents, but if you want a really big loaf of bread, it's twelve cents. She uses lard instead of olive oil because olive oil costs a lot and lard we get from the pork shop. It's okay and you get used to eating it.

Mom is saying, "I know it's hard working with Dad 'til all hours, but it won't be forever, Son."

"When we lived in Bayside, Mom, I was driven to school in a limo and I had real nice clothes. I remember Dad buyin' me a race car with the number '7' on it."

"Never mind Mr. Tough Guy, just read your books like your friend Lou!"

"Mom, Lou's got asthma, he's got to stay in and read."

....

At *PS 14 Elementary & Middle School* in *Corona Heights*, the school looks like it's been bombed. Tape is on all of the windows and graffiti is everywhere. Today the whole school is assembled in the school auditorium. The principal, Mrs. Sower, is at the podium. She is a tall, skinny redhead, very high-strung and nervous. She is yelling into the mike to get the attention of the audience of rowdy kids.

"Please may I have your attention! Please!!" The assembly quiets down. "Thank you . . . now, I have some exciting new changes to tell you about as they affect you here at *PS 14*. From this point forward, boys will take showers every Friday at second period."

The kids all giggle and snicker. "Quiet everyone, please! Listen. All the girls will now learn to sew every second period in Home Economics class and will have lessons on the grooming of their hair and nails on a daily basis. Also, I would like to introduce Mr. Bill Sadlo, our new Boxing Instructor who will keep the peace in our school and teach Gym, Health and Hygiene. Also at this time I want to introduce Herbert Bloomberg as Head Monitor of the Student Body. Herbert is one of our brightest students at *PS 14*. You will answer to Herbert for any infractions of the school rules and Herbert will answer to me in writing whenever a pupil is tardy or causes trouble of any kind."

There is mumbling and grumbling from the assembly. "Thank you for your attention students and we expect your cooperation on these issues. You may be dismissed to classes now." The kids are all noisy and rowdy as they leave the auditorium.

In the classroom, Frankie is sitting next to his best friend, Corky, and on the other side are their girlfriends, Antoinette and Julia. Wednesday is assembly day and the boys had to wear white shirts and the girls, white blouses. The teacher is trying to quiet the room.

"Children, please turn in your homework from Friday."

Mrs. Ork turns her back and begins writing on the blackboard. Corky and Frankie sneak out the back door to smoke and talk about the club Corky's in, *The Corona Dukes*. After the fight with Orlando, the guys all have respect for Frankie.

In the Boy's Restroom, Corky says, "No shit, we got the toughest and sharpest guys in the neighborhood. Rico, the oldest guy, went to *Sing Sing*. He tells us stories about the bad zootzoons and the happy queers. No kiddin' Frankie, it's really great bein' a *Duke* and we always help each other. Wednesdays we have a meetin'. You come with me and I'll okay you. You'll have no trouble makin' the grade. You got a lot of balls."

"All right Corky, I trust you . . . and we'll always be together."

The Corona Dukes clubhouse is a rented store with sofas and leather chairs, side tables and a tile floor. There is a large meeting table at the front of the room, a radio and a record player. The place is neat as a pin. A big stuffed Marlin is hanging on the wall with the caption underneath:

"This fish would still be swimming if he had kept his mouth shut"

The meeting of *The Corona Dukes* club is about to begin. A tall, well- built teen about 15 years old with dark, rough features is the leader and President of *The Dukes*. His name is Aldo. He calls the meeting to order.

"Okay, everybody sit and be quiet. Before we talk about our good and bad problems, Corky wants to bring in a new member. His name is Frankie 'Sonny' Basilio. Corky will be responsible for him. I met Frankie in school and I've seen him handle himself a coupl'a times. Before we vote, is there anybody who objects or has a beef against him?" Bobby Ferro raises his hand. Bobby has a "map of Italy" face. He's an average-size kid with a chip on his shoulder.

"He used to be rich, comes from *Bayside*. I bet he never went hungry. I don't know. You say he's okay, but he's gotta prove it to me before I vote for him."

Corky says, "Bobby, you wanna fight him outside right now? Would that make you feel better? He'd probably kick the shit outta ya."

Frankie asks to speak. "Lemme speak. I know I'm new in *Corona* and, yeah, my family was rich. But we lost 28 trucks, a half mile of sand, a rock crusher and a big house. Now I go with my father every morning before school to pick-up cardboard and any junk I can find or steal. The second thing . . . if you think I won't stand up to you or anybody else, then test me, okay?"

Aldo cuts in. "Okay you guys, anybody else got somethin' to say?" Nobody has anything else to say. Aldo begins telling Frankie the rules of the club. "These are the rules, Frankie: (1) No fighting in the club, (2) No reefers or cocaine allowed in or out of the club, (3) If you steal, you must share with the members, (4) Anyone who rats on anyone is out of the club, (5) Never talk about our club business to strangers and (6) Don't ever take the side of a girl or a stranger above a *Dukes* member."

Orlando, who is now Frankie's good friend and who wants to be a barber, is a real clown. He chimes in: "Hey Frankie, I'll vote for ya if you let me be your barber." Everybody laughs.

Aldo says, "Okay let's vote. 'Yes' he's in. 'No' he's out. Raise your hand for Yes". Everybody raises their hand – even Bobby. Frankie is humbled and thanks them all. The meeting is over and the guys all gather around Frankie with congratulations and "welcome". They're all firing questions at once, wanting to know how it feels to be rich . . . what kind of clothes rich kids wear . . .

Corky says to Frankie, Orlando and Aldo, "C'mon guys, let's go to Spaghetti Park. Maybe we can hustle a coupl'a Lemon Ices.". . .

....

Spaghetti Park is a two block triangle between Corona Avenue on one side and 108th Street on the other. There are park benches, trees, shrubs and a water fountain in the center. It is neat as a pin, no trash anywhere and not a scratch on any of the benches. The park is overseen by a "Street Boss" and only "neighborhood" people are allowed. Any problems and you got to go see the Street Boss. His word is law. Old men sit in the park and play cards and bullshit about the President and the war. Mussolini is a main topic of conversation.

The old Italian men all look alike with their plaid shirts, grey or brown sweaters and *De Nobili* cigars hanging out of their mouths. At the end of Corona Avenue and 108th Street is "Nicholes Lemon Ice King" which has been there forever. Any flavor you want, he's got it . . . but it's still called "Lemon" Ice.

Aldo tells Frankie, "Go ahead, you know how to talk Italian to those old guys. Go ahead. Say somethin' like, '*Mussolini was a great guy, says he built all the roads in Italy*' . . . any fuckin' thing. They'll give us money for the Lemon Ices, capeesh?"

Frankie slowly walks over to the old men sitting on the park bench. "They wanna play '*Morra*'." He winks at his guys because he knows that the old men can't see as well as they used to. They begin playing the hand game and Frankie gives them a wrong count. They owe 3 cents and then 3 cents a few more times. After a few more hustles, Orlando says, "C'mon let's go. Let's get a Lemon Ice . . . It's funny. We get bigger and those guys shrink. I never seen a tall old man!"

Aldo says, "You're nuts, Orlando!"

A few days later, Frankie is in the park again talking with an old Italian guy. He says, "You kids today, you think you know things, but I'm gonna tell you a story. When we came to America from Italy, we were all laborers.

The Irish, they got here first and they became the conductors on the trains and the foremen because they spoke the English. The Italians were treated like shit. They'd say, 'C'mere Dago, c'mere you grease ball'. I knew four Italian guys who were working for a construction company pouring concrete. The Foreman on the job was an Irish guy. They're diggin' a big hole in the middle of the city to erect a monument. The guys get nothin' but abuse from this Irish bastard. He tells them, 'You damn Dago's get over here and get to work or I'll fire your asses.' They couldn't take the abuse anymore so they went back to the neighborhood to talk to the Street Boss.

"You gotta help us," they said.

The Street Boss says, "Whadya want? What's the matter?"

They tell him, *"The Foreman where we work is this Irish bastard that keeps yellin' and cursin' at us, tellin' us he's gonna fire us, threatening our families. He's makin' our lives miserable."*

"Well, whadya want me to do," says the Street Boss.

"Get rid of him. We don't want him around." *"Okay, you give me $250 and I'll handle it."*

They pool their money and a couple of days later they give the Street Boss the $250. He tells them, *"You go to work, mind your business and don't say nothin' to nobody. Just tell me when they're gonna bring in the hoppers to pour the concrete."*

The next day, the Italian guys go to the Street Boss and tell him, *"They're gonna bring in the hoppers on Thursday morning at 5AM."* *"Okay, I'll be there,"* he says.

On Thursday, the Street Boss is there dressed in overalls and working alongside the other laborers. The Irish Foreman is yelling at everybody, *"Hey you Dago's, get over here. Get your lazy Italian asses to work."* As soon as they pull the chute and the concrete starts pouring out, the Street Boss calls over to the Foreman, *"Hey, c'mere a minute."*

"What the hell do you want?" says the Irish Foreman as he walks over to the Street Boss who without any hesitation pushes him into the hole while the concrete immediately covers him over.

Frankie is fascinated by these stories and loves listening to them. The old Italian guys are called "The Moustache Crew" and most of them were wise guys at one time.

Another old-timer tells Frankie, "I'm gonna tell you another story. Two well-dressed men were walking down Fifth Avenue – not together – separately – and they bump into each other and get into an argument, making a scene on the street. One guy pulls out a gun and yells, *'You sonovabitch'* and he fires the gun. The other guy collapses on the sidewalk.

An onlooker says, *"Oh my God, call the police."*

The shooter says, *"No, no, you don't call the police if you know what's good for ya. You're a witness so ya know what I gotta do to you."*

The onlooker says, *"Okay, okay, I don't wanna be involved. I didn't see anything."*

The shooter says, "*Look, I'm gonna need some money to get outta town.*"

"*Well, how much do you need?*" "*Gimme $500.*"

So the guy gives him $500. The guy is yelling, "*I didn't see anything, I didn't see anything,*" as he runs off down the street.

Next thing you know, the guy layin' on the sidewalk gets up and the two of them walk away. Happens all the time, Frankie."

....

Fort Totten Army Base is about 15 miles from *Corona*. The soldiers on furlough come into *Corona* and fool around at the school dances. Frankie and his gang give them a beating for messing around with the girls in the neighborhood. They throw rocks at them, hitting them in the head. The army makes *Corona* "off limits" to all soldiers at Fort Totten.

....

It's Saturday afternoon at the Basilio home and Connie says to Frankie, "Are you going to the school yard to play basketball or do you wanna help me and Gramma put the Bobbie's on these cards?"

Gramma says, "Connie, let Frankie go with his friends. We can finish this batch tonight."

"Mom, do you know they made that Jew kid, Bloomberg, the Head Monitor at school? The Bloomberg's sure got it good. They own the lumber yard and his father is President of the Bank."

Connie angrily yells out, "That sonovabitch! . . . I'm sorry Frankie, but he's the bum that took our house in Bayside!" She starts to cry.

Gramma says, "Go, Frankie. Go play with your friends."

Frankie can't stand to see his mother crying and runs out of the house while Gramma consoles Connie.

....

At the basketball court, Frankie is talking to his guys. "I can't believe the principal made that fat bastard the Head Monitor. I'm gonna tell you guys somethin'. Herbie Bloomberg's father is the President of the Bank. He took our house in Bayside for himself. From now on every day after school, I'm gonna give Herbie a beatin' and I don't want nobody else involved. This is like they say in the movies, a 'vendetta'!" All the guys nod in agreement.

The following Monday at 3:00 PM outside school, word has gotten around that Frankie is going to fight Herbie Bloomberg. The kids make a circle around Frankie and they push Herbie into the circle. Frankie has a stick on his shoulder and tells Herbie to knock it off.

"I don't fight in my school clothes. And, besides, I didn't report you to the teacher, so what's the problem?"

"Knock the stick off my shoulder 'cause I'm gonna break your head," says Frankie. "The kids are all yelling and moving in, making the circle smaller. Herbie refuses to knock the stick off.

"The hell with the stick!" Frankie says. He swings and hits Herbie in the mouth. Herbie tries to hit back. Misses. Frankie is a natural with his hands. He hits Herbie again and he hits the ground. Kids are screaming, "Kick him! Bust his head!" When he gets up, Frankie hits him again. Herbie goes down again with blood all over his face. He gets up for the third time. Frankie punches him in the stomach. "This one is for your father!" One more to the stomach.

Someone in the crowd yells, "The cops are comin'!" The fight breaks up and Herbie runs towards his father's lumber yard. The Dukes walk back into the school yard. The cops just go cruising by.

....

At Spaghetti Park, Aldo says to the guys, "Now listen, tonight we're gonna rob Gebroules truck. He goes to sleep early. Frankie is gonna drive. We'll go to Rockaway Beach and get back before midnight. Orlando, you call the girls and be sure to get 'Crazy' Junior in case we get in a fight. He'd scare the shit outta anybody. Built like a fire hydrant. I saw him throw a guy through a store window in Flushing once. He's crazy!"

"I'm glad he's in our club", says Orlando. "Who's gonna fine him 25 cents for missin' a meetin'? Not me. I'm glad that's you, Aldo my boy - Mr. President!"

....

Gebroules is an old short guy with a big nose and a long forehead. He's not real smart and he's half blind. He has a junk business, but how the hell he drives a truck, no one knows. His truck is a beat up old Ford pick-up and it's always parked in the street in front of his house. Frankie steals it three or four nights a week. The guys wait on the corner while Frankie jumps in the truck, puts it in second gear, gives it a push and takes off. Frankie could drive since he was thirteen. He's the best driver in the neighborhood and no one else in the club can drive. If they don't have a "job" to pull or nothing else to do, they go joy riding in Gebroules truck.

Gebroules hangs out almost every night in front of the Grocery Store on the corner. Frankie drives right by him on the street and Corky says, "Whadya doin' Frankie?!"

"It's okay, don't worry. Just watch this . . . hey Gebroules, how ya doin'?" asks Frankie.

"Uh, uh, okay kid, how you doin'? You all right?"

"Yeah, I'm okay," says Frankie, and he pulls away with everybody laughing hysterically.

"You crazy bastard," says Corky. "How could you pull right up in front of him in his own fuckin' truck?"

"Don't worry about it. He can't see nothin'."

....

Milano's Market is the name of the corner Store at 108th Street owned by Freddie and Dora, a Jewish couple. Corky and Frankie go in the store every week and do the same routine every time: Corky looks around while Frankie grabs Dora who is a fat little Jewish lady about fifty years old. She loves it when Frankie comes in because he grabs her, walks her into the back room and plays with her tits. She says, "Ohhhh Frankie, please don't do that. Stop it honey. Oh, you're so cute."

Meanwhile, Corky steals soda and chips and anything else he can grab. When they get ready to leave, Dora says, "Oh Frankie, you're so nice, so sweet."

Frankie pinches her cheek. He asks her, "Where's Freddie tonight?" Dora's husband, Freddie, is a weird little Jewish guy. He tells everyone that he's Italian.

Frankie asks Dora, "Is it true that Freddie has a wooden dick?" (The neighborhood joke is that Freddie never fucks his wife and has a wooden dick.)

She says, "Oh no, no."

"Well, that's what we heard."

They run out of the store with Dora laughing, thinking that Frankie has made a funny joke.

A few days later, Frankie's Mama tells him, "Go down to Milano's and buy 15 cents worth of cold cuts. Tell Dora to put it on the bill." Dora keeps a ledger book on the counter and writes in it: "Frankie's mama wants 15 cents of cold cuts – did not pay". There is always a balance of three or four dollars and Dora says, "Frankie, you gotta pay the bill."

"Ah, c'mon Dora." Frankie pinches her cheek and she says, "Okay, okay sweet Frankie. You come back, you pay next time."

....

Frankie is behind the wheel of Gebroules truck. He is wearing a hat like his dad does to try to look older. He's only a kid, but he's a good driver - never goes through any red lights and never speeds. The hand-painted sign on the door of the truck reads: *Gebroules Trucking Co.* The truck pulls into a gas station with six kids in the back and three up front. Everybody is "taxed" a nickel or a dime for gas. Six gallons cost 60 cents. If the girls don't have the money, the boys pat them on the ass, laughing, and say, "Don't worry about it, you could pay us later."

Aldo tells Frankie, "Before we go to Rockaway, drive to White Castle and let's get six hamburgers. It'll cost us a quarter."

"Good idea, Aldo . . . yesterday, Orlando and me sold Miguel, the Junkman, some copper. Robbed it back that night and sold it again this morning! We'll get plenty of hamburgers."

....

At Rockaway Beach, Corky, Frankie, Aldo, Orlando, Junior and the girls, Millie, Julia, Antoinette and Margie from Maspeth are all hanging out. Aldo says to Frankie, "Margie takes on all the Corona Dukes a coupl'a times a week and she loves it, so we treat her real good! Rest of the girls say they gotta be in love - what bullshit!"

Corky, pointing to Julia says, "I gotta hump that chick tonight!"

Frankie tells Corky, "Don't be a putz and get the girls mad at us. They'll stop doin' our homework and we'll never graduate! Anyway Corky, just grab Margie when your turn comes, okay?"

They put a blanket down on the sand with everything on top of it and Frankie says, "Junior, you stay here and watch this stuff in case anybody comes around."

Junior says, "Whadya think I am, a cop? I wanna go in the water too."

"No, you stay here and guard the stuff, Junior. Nobody's gonna mess with you."

Junior decides to make a fire. "You'll freeze your balls off comin' outta the water. . . Hey, after I hump Margie, we better get goin' though. It's gettin' late and my mother can't sleep 'til I get home."

Frankie is in the water with Antoinette and he feels something brush his leg. He thinks it's a log or something, but it's a dead guy just floating by on the water. Everybody is scared shitless as they all run out of the water with Frankie yelling, "Let's get the fuck outta here."

....

After graduation from *PS 14*, Frankie and Corky enter *Newtown High.* Frankie is able to select some classes and he picks "M.D." (Mechanical Drawing). He has absolutely no idea what that is and he can't draw a straight line with a ruler. The teacher, Mr. Lebron, is a chubby little guy with a nervous condition, the kind of guy only a mother could love. Frankie and Corky sit in the back of the classroom and smoke.

"Okay, that's it you two hoodlums! I'm reporting you to Principal Hagen for smoking in class."

Outside the principal's office is a cage with a lock on the door. Inside the cage are a desk and a chair. Frankie and Corky are often bored in class and pay absolutely no attention to Mr. Lebron. After the smoking incident, they are sent to the "Cage".

In Woodworking class, the teacher Mr. Adams sets out tools and planks of wood for the students. Frankie and Corky throw the wood on the floor and start playing catch with the tools, disrupting the whole class. All the kids laugh. Mr. Adams tells Frankie and Corky, "You boys are going to flunk this class if you continue this behavior and don't start paying attention!" They are again sent to the "Cage".

The next day, Frankie and Corky go early to Woodworking class. Frankie picks up a saw and begins sawing the legs of Mr. Adams' wooden chair about half-way through the legs. When the teacher enters and sits down at his desk, the class watches as the chair breaks and Mr. Adams hits the floor. Everyone is laughing hysterically. The teacher says, "I demand to know which one of you did this!" No one dares to come forward.

In English class, Frankie and Corky have girlfriends who do their homework for them every day. Antoinette is Frankie's girl and Corky goes with Julia. They are smart girls. Frankie and Corky turn in English papers and get B's, much to the surprise of the teacher. They pass English.

Mr. Mayer is the Arithmetic teacher. He's real cocky until Frankie gets up out of his seat and gives him a "look". If you're failing in Arithmetic, you can't play sports. Every Friday afternoon during fourth period, the boys play basketball or softball. Every kid waits for Friday. Frankie and Corky are both failing in Arithmetic and Mr. Mayer tells them, "You two bums can't play." Frankie turns to Corky and says, "Hey, Cork, open that window, will ya?" The classroom is four stories high. Frankie and Rinaldo, another tough guy in class, grab Mr. Mayer and hang him out the window by his feet. Rinaldo yells, "Hey, he's shittin' his pants!" . . . Mr. Mayer gives Frankie and Corky passing grades in Arithmetic so they can now play sports on Fridays.

Eventually, Principal Hagen hears about the "window" incident and Frankie, Corky and Rinaldo are all suspended from school. Corky and Frankie decide to find a way to get back at Principal Hagen who is also the Boy Scout Master. Frankie and his pals often go swimming in the river, playing hooky from school, and Principal Hagen sends his Boy Scout Troop after them. "Hey guys, here comes those fuckin' Boy Scouts," says Frankie. "Let's throw 'em in the river." Two more times and the principal stops sending the troop and Frankie and Corky are officially expelled from Newtown High. They are not yet sixteen years old and have to go to Queens Vocational School.

....

The Irish cop on the neighborhood beat is a big fat guy by the name of O'Sullivan. He's so fat he's busting out of his uniform. He dribbles all the time and drool is constantly running down the sides of his mouth. Whenever he sees Frankie and his guys on the corner, he says, "*You damn Dago kids get the hell off the streets. What are you doin' in America anyway, you Wops?*"

Frankie is tired of his abuse and tells Corky and Orlando, "I'm gonna straighten his ass out."

On the corner is a stand-up phone booth which O'Sullivan uses to call his wife. While he is in the phone booth, Frankie and the guys sneak around the back of the booth with a big heavy chain that they wrap around the booth and hook up to a pick-up truck. They jump in the truck and take off. The phone booth falls over and they pull it down the street with O'Sullivan rolling over and over, yelling, "You mother fuckers!" They eventually stop, unhook the chain and take off . . .

The next time they see O'Sullivan, he says "Top'a the mornin' boys. How ya doin'?" Like nothing ever happened.

....

Aldo, Frankie, Orlando and Junior are in the *Corona Dukes* clubhouse planning on robbing the new apartment building that's under construction, but just about to be completed. Aldo says, "We can rob the stoves and refrigerators and all the copper gutters, even the sinks if they're still in the crates, okay?"

Frankie says, "Okay, but that means I gotta rob Gebroules truck again to haul the stuff off, right?

"Yeah, that's right, Frankie," says Aldo.

Frankie tells everybody, "I talked to Irv the Jew and he said he would buy the whole truckload of swag: the stoves, refrigerators, all the copper gutters, tool boxes, rolls of carpet, whatever we get."

"How much is he gonna pay us?" asks Junior.

"I said $500 cash, okay?" says Frankie. "He said he wants it delivered to his warehouse."

"What if he backs off the price and tries to hustle us?"

"He won't like the results. Maybe his wife won't recognize him in the hospital. Junior, don't worry. I promise he'll pay," says Frankie.

"Okay then," says Junior. "Aldo, your job is to climb up on the roof and pull the copper off. You're strong and you move like a cat. Then you jump down and I'll catch you. Don't worry."

Frankie says, "We could sell the stuff to Miguel too and then rob it back!"

Aldo tells everybody, "Okay, let's plan it for Wednesday night after the meeting. Don't tell anyone else about it. If we score good, we'll buy club jackets with our names on the front and 'Corona Dukes' on the back. We all get one."

Orlando says, "Ya know, since Wednesday night is our robbing night, let's stop by 'Rocky the Barber' and grab one of his barber chairs and then I'll give y'all free haircuts for three months." They all laugh.

....

At the corner of 111th Street and 48th Avenue stands a beautiful new two-story apartment house, dark and empty. The landscaping is not yet done, but it's ready to move into. Gebroules truck pulls into the yard with the lights off. Frankie and Aldo are in the front and Orlando and Junior are in the back.

Orlando and Junior get out and take a look around. They come back saying, "Let's get started." Frankie has his arm covered with burlap and breaks the glass on the rear door of the building. Junior runs in and picks up a crate with a new stove in it and puts it in the truck. Orlando and Frankie are sliding a refrigerator over to the truck. Aldo is already on the roof, tearing copper gutter off and dropping it carefully onto the dirt below. In less than 15 minutes, the truck is loaded and on its way to Irv the Jew's warehouse.

Back at Spaghetti Park, Orlando says, "Man, we sure work good together! Maybe I won't be a barber after all. I think I'll be a robber!"

Aldo asks Junior, "How did you carry that heavy stove by yourself and then catch me jumpin' off the roof? You're like an ox! . . . hey, here comes Frankie. Let's go collect our scratch from Irv."

....

The Basilio family is sitting down to dinner and Joe is talking with Connie. "What's goin' on with Sonny? I'm workin' twelve hours a day and I never see him anymore."

"He'll be here any minute, Joe. He ran to the store for me. Ya know, Joe, Sonny's changed – he's not a little kid anymore. All the girls in the neighborhood say he's so big and handsome. Eleanor's niece has a real crush on Sonny – too bad she's married and a little older than him."

"A little older!" says Gramma. "She's 31 years old and she's a *poutanna*! My sweet grandson, Sonny, nice'a boy, looks like Frank Sinatra."

The kitchen door opens and Frankie walks in with the dry cleaning.

"Hey Dad, how you doin'? I want you to take it easy and don't worry about money. I give Mom plenty."

"Plenty? From where? Where do you get the money? You're in high school, Sonny, for Christ's sake. They pay you to go to school nowadays?" Joe picks up the newspaper.

"C'mon Dad, I got a part-time job as a waiter at the pizza joint. I do all right. Maybe someday soon I'll buy the joint and you can run it . . . C'mon Ma, let's eat. I got a date.

....

It's a cool September night. The lamp post light is just enough to see the spots on the dice. There are five guys in a circle shooting craps. You can hear the quarters and half-dollars hitting the asphalt and Frankie is saying, "Who wants to fade this deuce?" After all, it's his game. His partner, Corky, makes change, but Frankie's mind isn't on the game this night. He keeps looking across the street at a green Ford with this wild looking chick patiently waiting for him. The game lasts another hour and, as usual, Frankie and Corky end up with most of the money. "Their Game" means cut a quarter from each pot. Between that and robbing the plumber's warehouse two or three times a week, they're living pretty well for guys of 16.

．．．．．．．．．．．．．．．．．．．．．．．

Aldo's mother's name is Eleanor Pucci. Her house in *Corona Heights* has three bedrooms, is plainly decorated with simple furniture, but is immaculately clean. The kitchen is the biggest in the neighborhood and Eleanor's friends like to gather there to bake. Today, Connie Basilio is here with Gramma Basilio, baking cookies together and talking about the up-coming Feast of the Virgin Mary.

"We gotta make money for the Church," says Connie. "How do you think we can do it? What if we bake these cookies, some *anisette*, *biscotti's*? I wish it to be the best Feast ever, to honor the Virgin!"

As they talk, they are cutting cookies from the dough on the cutting board in the middle of the kitchen. Eleanor is getting the cookie sheets ready to pop into the oven. Gramma is sifting more flour.

"I'll make gravy," says Gramma. "But I wish there was enough money for pork, enough for sausage in the gravy. We would make money selling sausage sandwiches for a good price."

Eleanor says, "I'll ask Aldo and his friends to have a raffle and maybe raise money for us to buy food that we could sell at the feast . . . but, we have to hurry now and get this last batch done or we'll be late to the Church."

....

Aldo, Frankie, Orlando and Junior are playing basketball in the school yard. They take sides. Ten points wins.

Aldo says, "You know my mother and Frankie's mother was talkin' about the feast. They want us to have a raffle to raise money for the Church."

Frankie says, "Orlando, you're good with people. Go around and sell tickets for 25 cents apiece, $2.50 a book. If they say no, tell 'em we'll break their windows or their heads!"

Junior pipes up, "I got an idea! You know the pig farm in Elmhurst? Let's go one night and rob a pig. We can cook him and that way the ladies will have plenty of pork for the gravy and sliced pork for the sandwiches. They could make sausage."

"*Madone*! That pig farm stinks like a bastard!" says Orlando.

"Junior, we can get a big burlap bag and stick the pig in that, but you gotta pick the pig up and put it over the fence. Aldo and I will help. Frankie will drive Gebroules truck."

"You guys must think it's my truck," says Frankie. "Gebroules is gonna be waitin' in the dark some night and shoot me! Is that what you want?"

The guys all groan. "Yeah sure, Frankie, ya know he can't see worth a shit!"

"Okay, okay, I'll do it," says Frankie.

Late the next night at the *Elmhurst Pig Farm*, Aldo tells Junior, "Remember, find a nice big fat one then throw the bag over his head. Lift him up so Orlando and I can put him in the truck. He'll squeal like hell. Don't be scared, but be quick so the farmer don't start shootin' at us!"

Junior climbs over the fence. "Ych, ych . . . damn shit! I'm steppin' in pig shit! Ughhhhh, it stinks!! I slipped on my ass and now I'm full'a pig shit! . . . come here, you hairy bastard!"

Frankie says, "Junior, stop talkin' to the fuckin' pigs and grab one! Hurry up!"

Orlando tells him, "Hey, don't kiss the pig. You can do that later!" They all laugh.

Junior yells, "I got one! . . . you dirty fuckin' pig! Get in the bag . . . that's it. Watch out, here comes the squealin' bastard!"

Orlando and Aldo grab the pig over the fence and put it in the truck.

Junior is full of shit and stinks like a pig. Aldo says, "Tie the rope around the bag and hurry up before he gets loose!"

"Hey, I'm not ridin' in the back with those two pigs!" says Orlando. "C'mon let me ride with you Aldo. I'm gonna throw up! I mean it!! I swear to God!!!"

Frankie says, "Orlando, shut up! It's for a good cause. It's for the Church. Just sit in the corner away from Junior and the pig. I've gotta bring Gebroules truck back. Aldo, you got a back yard, we'll bring the pig there."

"Are you crazy, Frankie! My mother sees a pig, she'll faint . . . ah shit, guess nobody else has a back yard. Okay, bring the hairy bastard to my yard. But what am I gonna tell my mother? '*Junior found a pig*' '*the pig was hitchhikin'*'. C'mon you guys, help me lie."

The next day in Eleanor Pucci's kitchen, Eleanor, Connie and Gramma are having coffee and cake. Eleanor says, "I woke up this morning and heard squealing in the back yard. There's this fat hairy pig running around, snorting and squealing. I know our kids are a little crazy and do the darndest things, but a pig, a big fat pig?! . . . Aldo left a note last night, saying he was sleeping over at Frankie's house."

"I know," says Connie. "Those two bums were snoring this morning and the bedroom stunk! Now I know why."

"C'mon, they're good kids," says Gramma. "Maybe we're gonna have a roasted pig in time for the feast? In Italy, we always cooked a pig on holidays. My dear husband, rest his soul, he would come home with a nice fat pig. He said he 'got a bargain'. I know he lied, but the pig was delicious!"

Later that day in Eleanor Pucci's back yard all of the *Corona Dukes* are chasing the pig around the yard. Aldo asks, "Who's gonna kill the pig? Frankie, do you wanna shoot him?"

"You can't shoot the pig", says Frankie. The lead will poison the meat . . . Petey, you kill him - with a big rock to the head."

Petey says, "Are you nuts? Their skin is six inches thick. Junior, you're strong. Choke the fuckin' pig."

"Hey, I'm not that strong," says Junior, "and besides, I like the pig. He's got balls. Who's gonna kill him? Not me!"

Gramma appears from the back stoop. "I hear all you sissies sayin' you don't wanna kill'a the pig. This is for the Church! Get me a big knife and you sissies grab the pig by each ear. Junior, you sit on top and hold his head up."

Aldo is dumbfounded, but hands Gramma a big sharp kitchen knife. "Okay," says Gramma, "hold the pig tight, Junior. You boys grab his ears and pull his head up high." The pig is squealing and trying to get loose. With the skill of a surgeon, Gramma slits the pig's throat first one way and then the other. Blood is squirting out all over. "Good boys. Hold him 'til he falls down or he'll have blood all over the yard."

Junior is pale as a ghost and Orlando starts to vomit. Aldo and Frankie are in shock, still holding the pig. Gramma is steady as a rock, holding the bloody knife. "Give me a towel to wipe'a my hands," she says. She looks up at the sky and murmurs a prayer in Italian.

....

All the blocks on the streets in *Corona* are closed to cars. It is the day of the Feast of the Virgin Mary. Stands are set-up selling ice cream, pizza, sausage and peppers and roast pork sandwiches. *The Corona Dukes* have shaken down every merchant in the neighborhood. There were a few broken windows, but, hey, it was for the Church!

There are lots of pretty girls at the feast, but only neighborhood guys can dance with them. Everybody else can eat and drink, but no messin' with the girls!

Gramma is at a stand selling sausage and pepper sandwiches. She is the most respected person in the neighborhood now including the Street Boss.

....

As the feast came and went, so did the years . . .

Herbie Bloomberg got tired of taking beatings from Frankie every day. His mother and father said,

"This is no place for us to raise our son!" They evict the tenants who are renting the old Basilio house in *Bayside* and move themselves in. Nobody hears from them again . . .

The Corona Dukes always manage to stay one step ahead of the law. They learn how to make pay-offs to the cops so they won't be bothered anymore.

Frankie has to fight two to three times a week to get the prestige to be the top guy in his crew. Eddie "Lab" (short for Labriota) is what they call a "made guy". Fifty-some years old, he likes Frankie and says, "Look Frankie, you're a ballsy kid and not only that, you're the only guy I know that's got green eyes. Everybody in Corona's got brown eyes, but you, you got green eyes. I don't understand where the hell you came from."

Frankie laughs and says, "Well, you heard of Frank Sinatra? He's got blue eyes and he's Italian too." They both laugh.

Eddie says, "I'm gonna put a little responsibility on you, Frankie. I want you goin' around collecting from four different places. You pick up the numbers and bring 'em in and that'll be your start. I'm gonna teach you the bookmakin' business and I'm gonna teach you how to take horse bets. You know how kids go to school and when they wanna become doctors they gotta graduate from Medical school? Well, as you move up, I'll help graduate you." He laughs. "I'm gonna make you a Street Boss, a hoodlum like me, Frankie, because you got the balls to do it."

Frankie says, "Okay, I'll do whatever you want." He does a good job picking up numbers. Soon, Frankie and other guys of his rank and stature have to pool their money to pay off the cops: $50 a week goes to the cop on the beat, $200 a week to the Precinct Captain and $500 a month is paid for the use of the telephones; all this so they can operate freely and nobody gets locked up.

Frankie starts bringing in a lot of money for a kid. He gives it to his

Mom and says, "Here, take this, Mom."

She says, "No, Frankie. How'd you get it?" "I won it in a crap game, Mom."

....

Papa Joe likes to get up in the morning and make eggs for everybody. They have an old beat up stove so Frankie goes out and buys the best estate stove he can find and has it delivered. It cost $500. When the delivery man arrives, Joe answers the door, sees the stove and nearly passes out. He says, "This isn't my stove. Get it outta here."

The delivery guy says, "No, it's your stove. It's paid for." He sets it in the kitchen, hooks it up and leaves.

When Frankie comes home, Joe says, "Frankie, what is this? Where'd this stove come from?"

"Dad, I bought you a stove. It's nothin'. You like to make eggs – make eggs."

"Where'd you get the money, Frankie?"

"Don't worry about it, Dad. I won it in a crap game."

"I don't want that kinda money, Frankie. Take the damn stove back."

....

Frankie and Gramma are at home in the kitchen. Gramma has ordered some groceries to be delivered and Frankie is on his way to the bathroom. He says, "Here Gramma, when the delivery guy comes with the groceries give him this money." He hands Gramma some bills and goes into the bathroom. There's a knock at the door and Gramma goes to answer it. Frankie hears a loud, deep, gravelly voice say, "Lady, this bill is $3.95." Gramma gives him the money and there's a nickel left over as a tip. In the same loud, deep, gravelly voice the guy says, "What, are you crazy lady!"

Frankie hears him and runs out of the bathroom saying, "You can't yell at my Gramma like that, you rat bastard!" He hits the guy and he falls down the stairs. Frankie drags him out to the gravel side yard. He's yelling and screaming and Frankie says, "You ever yell at my Gramma in my house like that again, I'll leave ya for dead." The guy looks at Frankie and says, "I'm not raising my voice. This is how I talk. Everybody's after me just 'cause I have a heavy voice." Frankie takes out twenty bucks and says, "Here, put this in your pocket, I'm sorry."

"You people are all crazy! You Italian people are all the same!" And he runs off.

....

The string of stores along Main Street in *Flushing* consists of a drug store, a tailor shop, a corner market, a Bar & Food Tavern and a boarded- up fish market.

Uncle Pete spotted the empty Fish Store some time ago. In addition to Connie giving Pete her diamond ring, Frankie put up money for the rents to get the store opened. Nobody in the family knows anything about fish or running a fish store. The closest thing to fishing any of them has done is when Pete goes fishing at Whitestone Beach and catches little Keelies.

Uncle Pete says, "I don't know nothin' about fish."

Frankie says, "Don't worry about it. Just get the store opened."

"Papa Joe's Fish Market" finally opens and people start coming in. Joe and Pete go each morning to Fulton Fish Market to buy the fish. Frankie, Joey and little Petey help out in the store when they're not in school.

....

The guys are having their weekly meeting at the clubhouse and Frankie is speaking, "Meekia, this war is a bitch! That's all ya hear about. We gotta stick together guys. Corky and me we nailed a truck full'a nylon stockings and some silk dresses. We sold 'em to Irv the Jew and cut up $2500. We got some other stuff comin' up. If you're in, that's it, no pullin' out. Whadya say?"

Orlando says, "That's big-time shit. I gotta think about it, Frankie, okay? I get caught, who's gonna look out for my mom, ya know what I mean?"

"Don't worry about it, Orlando, we understand," says Corky. "It's just that me and Frankie we gotta know where we stand."

Aldo says, "Listen, I'm older than you guys and I'm gonna get drafted in the fuckin' army soon. I'm sick of shinin' shoes. I'll probably get killed in the war anyway. Sonny . . . Corky . . . I'm in.

………………………..

Frankie and Corky are meeting in Chapman's Diner. "What's wrong, Frankie? You look upset. Did I fuck up?"

"No Cork, but that Irish dick saw me Tuesday night when we robbed the truck. You were already in the car, but he spotted me. Yesterday, he came over'ta my house. Good thing only Gramma was home. He wants to know who I was with and how much we scored. I told him to go fuck himself and he hit me with the sap. Like a jerk, I laughed and called him a leech. I caught another shot and it hurt like hell. He wants a $100 a week from me and a $100 from 'my partner' or I go to the can."

"Jesus Christ, Frankie, what are ya gonna do? You wanna kill the bastard? I'll do it with ya, Pal."

"Corky, we can't kill a cop. They'll hurt our families if we get nailed. We'll find a way. We're 17 – let's join the army."

"Are you nuts, Frankie? I don't wanna fight Japs. We can't even rob 'em. Anyway, my mother won't sign – no way!"

"You don't have to go, Corky. He didn't see you and he'll never know about you. Me, I gotta go or he'll make a whore outta me – hangin' that over my head for the rest of my life, you understand?"

"Frankie, are ya sure you ain't 25 years old instead of 17? Aren't you even scared to go overseas and be away from home?" Corky grabs Frankie and hugs him.

"C'mon Corky, it ain't the end of the world . . ."

……………………..

At the Induction Center on Whitehall Street, a group of people are standing and saying their goodbyes to each other. Moms and Pops have tears in their eyes and the girls are giving their heroes kisses before they go off to war. Corky says, "Jesus Frankie, you're really goin' away. I can't believe it. Ya know I feel real bad about this shit. We been partners since we was kids."

"For Christ Sake, stop worryin', Cork. I need the change anyway. Who knows, maybe I'll come back a hero."

"Up that cop's ass! Maybe he'll get killed by the time you get back, eh pal?" Frankie picks up his bag and starts walking away. "See ya Corky."

CHAPTER FOUR

All the new guys are in the barracks at Fort Dix, New Jersey for processing, but haven't been given uniforms yet. There's a group of guys with Italian names and they're sitting together talking. Ralphie Asiego is from Brooklyn. He's 5 ft. 8, skinny with a big nose and crooked teeth.

On the other side of the room, a tall Jewish kid named Appel is reading a comic book on a cot, and Ralphie tells him, "Gimme the comic book."

Appel says, "No, I'm reading it."

"I said, gimme the book . . . you're not gonna gimme the book?"

"No," says Appel.

Both of them stand up. Ralphie picks up a butt can full of sand, empties the sand on the floor, walks over and hits Appel in the face with the can, ripping open his cheek and ear. Appel falls on the floor, screaming like a banshee and bleeding all over the place. All the guys are yelling and cheering when the Sergeant walks in and yells, "What's all the commotion in here?"

Ralphie says, "I wanted the comic book and he wouldn't give it'a me so I hit him with the can."

"Are you nuts? You're in the army! You guys just got here - don't even have uniforms yet. Let's all just take it easy and try and get along, okay? Can you do that?" With that, the Sergeant walks out.

Somebody asks, "You guys all tough guys?"

Ralphie says, "Yeah."

"Where you guys from?"

Ralphie says, "I'm from Brooklyn. These other guys are from Corona, Harlem and downtown New York. And we're all together and that's the way it is."

Across the room, another guy stands up on his cot, puffs up his chest, flexes his muscles and says in a Southern redneck drawl, "You Italians are all full'a shit." (He pronounces it, "Sheee-it".)

Ralphie looks at Frankie. "Do you believe this rebel mother fucker?"

Frankie walks up to the guy, pulls him off the top bunk and hits him in the mouth. He's bleeding and yelling as the Sergeant walks back in and says, "Okay, who's the toughest guy in here?"

Ralphie points at Frankie and says, "He's the toughest guy in the place."

The Sergeant pulls out an armband with two stripes on it and says, "Okay tough guy, this is a Corporal's Armband and you're in charge in here." He hands the Armband to Frankie and says, "I don't want no more trouble, understood?"

Later, everyone is in line to get uniforms and the guy behind Frankie says, "Hey, my mom buys all my clothes. I don't even know what size I wear."

Frankie tells him, "You're just a little bigger than me, so just say one size more than I say."

They move up the line and Frankie says, "Size 9 shoe."

The guy says, "Gimme a 10."

Frankie says, "Neck 16."

The guy says, "Neck 17."

Frankie says, "Underwear large."

The guy says, "Underwear extra-large."
Frankie says, "Hat size six and seven eighths." The
guy says, "Hat 9-10-11." Everyone laughs.

....

Two weeks later, Frankie and Ralphie are in the
PX at Fort Jackson, South Carolina. Frankie is talking to
1st Sgt. Hall, a Tennessee rebel with the 82nd Airborne.
Sgt. Hall is big and tough with a chest full of medals and
ribbons.

"Hey boy, who'd you bribe to get into this here
Army? Is it true that all Italian gangsters are in New
York and Chicago (he pronounces it "Cheecago"). Shit
boy, you the most piss poor soldier I ever seen."

"C'mon Sarge, you never had shoes 'til you got in
the army. The only time you ever have a good meal is
when my mom sends us a package. You like ravioli and
meat balls, eh? Don't worry, Italians take care of their
friends – even though you rebels can't even talk
English."

"Damn boy, I'm glad there ain't many G.I.'s like you. Shit, we'd lose the damn war. I sure get a kick outta ya though, Frankie."

While in basic training, Frankie's mama sends packages of food from home: jars of macaroni, gravy, ravioli, salami, provolone, all packed into a big box. Frankie takes a butt can and puts charcoal and paper in it to make a fire to heat up whatever Mama has sent.

Sgt. Hall says, "Whadya doin', you gonna burn the place down!" "C'mon over here, Sarge, taste this."

Sgt. Hall takes a taste. "God damn, boy, you Italians sure know how to eat!" The Sergeant thinks Frankie is a wacko, but he likes him.

He asks Frankie, "Whadya wanna do in this here Army?" "I wanna jump outta planes."

"You wanna be a Paratrooper, huh?" "Yeah," says Frankie, "I'm not afraid."

The next day Frankie is getting into a harness and is being raised in the air to a platform from which he will be dropped 40 feet. He says, "Fuck this! I don't wanna do this, it's not for me."

The Sergeant says, "Well, Goddamn, you can't do this anyway boy, you got flat feet. You're goin' in the Infantry." (This is, of course, contrary to actual Army Policy regarding flat feet.)

Frankie says, "What the hell do I care. I don't give a shit where you put me."

....

The Infantry Sergeant tells his Platoon that they are going out on 15 mile night marches. It is really cold during basic training and Frankie looks at Ralphie and says, "Is this guy crazy? A 15 mile hike! Whadya think we got cars for? I'm not walkin' 15 miles and freeze my ass off."

"Frankie, you're in the fuckin' army, you gotta do it." "No way, Ralphie. Watch what I do."

"Whadya gonna do?"

Frankie says, "I got it all planned."

That night after all the guys put on their field gear, the Platoon sets out on a 15 mile march. As soon as they start to walk, Frankie begins counting under his breath and when he gets to 300 he falls on the ground.

The Sergeant hollers, "Company Halt. Medic! Medic!"

The medics rush over. Frankie is lying on the ground and says, "I can't walk anymore. My feet are killing me! I don't know what's wrong with me." He's crying like a baby.

The Sergeant says, "Get the jeep!" The medics get the jeep and take Frankie away. At Sick Bay, the doc exams him and says, "I don't see anything wrong with your feet."

Frankie says, "I got such bad feet, Doc, you have no idea."

He is sent back to the barracks and is lying on his cot smiling when Ralphie comes in from the long march.

After that, every time the Platoon goes out on a march, Frankie starts to count under his breath as soon as they start walking and when he gets to 300 he falls down. And every time, they take him to sick bay.

Captain Smith calls Frankie in and says, "Listen, you realize you're a goof-off? You're the worst soldier I've ever run into. I know what you do on those marches. You go to a certain place and you fall down."

"No Captain, I got bad feet."

"With your behavior and the trouble you cause – always fighting with somebody – I may give you a BCD."

Frankie asks, "What's a BCD?"

"A Bad Conduct Discharge," says the Captain.

"No sir, Captain Sir, I'm a good guy. I don't bother nobody. I can't go home with a BCD. I'll do whatever you want."

Captain Smith tells Frankie, "I'm gonna give you another chance to straighten your life out. But if you don't shape up, I'm gonna send you home with a BCD."

Frankie can't make it as a Paratrooper and he's not going to be an Infantryman, so he is now in the Medical Corp.

....

A clean-cut kid who looks like he should still be in high school tells Frankie, "I gotta go home. I can't stand it here!" His name is Danny Depollo and he is from somewhere in Massachusetts. He continues, "I need you to do me a favor, Frankie. Listen, I'm gonna go in my barracks and I'm goin' in the kitchen and stick my hands in hot grease. I'm gonna burn my hands and I need you to call the MP's and tell 'em that there's a guy goin' crazy here and that his hands are burning and they need to come right away. Will ya do that for me?"

Frankie says, "Sure, I'll do it."

Depollo says, "Okay, then they'll send me out on a medical discharge. Thanks buddy."

Later, after Frankie has made the call, an MP comes into Frankie's barracks and asks, "Where the hell's that Depollo kid that burned his damn hands? The stupid sonovabitch stuck his hands in hot grease.

Everybody says, "Really? Oh my God!"

Frankie says, "Well shouldn't you take care of it?"

The MP says, "I don't give a shit about him. He's not even in my Platoon. Let him call another MP from his own Platoon."

....

Frankie and Sgt. Hall are talking and Frankie says, "Well Sarge, I'll be goin' home on furlough in a few weeks then I'm goin' to Korea. Are you sure you can handle this Platoon without me?"

"Shit boy, this here place will be normal again once you gone."

....

Home on furlough from the army, Frankie hears a car pull up outside and he runs down to meet his pal, Corky, who he hasn't seen in almost two months.

"Mom, I'll see ya later. Corky's here and we're goin' out for a while."

"Sonny, it gets dark early, so you be careful and don't come home late."

Gramma tells Connie, "*Congetta*, keep'a quiet. Sonny, he's in the army and he's a big boy now."

Frankie gets in the car with Corky and tells him, "Oh man, it's good to see ya Cork and it's good to be home! I hate the Army! I can't take it much longer.

And now I gotta go overseas and I don't know what's gonna happen."

"Frankie listen, I've made some strong connections with some good people while you were gone. We got a connection with Bush Terminal at the Waterfront Pier. My guy is in charge and all we gotta do is pull our trucks in there, load 'em up with whatever swag comes in on the boats and give the guy an envelope on the way out . . . you know I didn't get this for nothin', Frankie. I had to earn it, capeesh? Oh, and I go to the big games now – one in Harlem, one in Long Island and also the Midtown game. I'll introduce you to some people. We'll be in action before you know it. I got a bankroll, so don't worry about it, okay partner?"

"Okay partner," says Frankie.

Pulling up to a large, dark building in Harlem, they park the car, get out and walk up to the massive steel front door. There are bars on the door and a buzzer to the right. Corky pushes the buzzer and a small window in the door opens. The guy behind the window recognizes Corky and buzzes him in. Inside, it looks like a Las Vegas casino. There are large banquet tables loaded with food and beverages served by waiters. People are crammed around the two crap tables and four blackjack tables in the center of the

96

room. Between the games is a step-up platform where a guy sits and watches the action – loaded for bear.

The top guy, Ralph, owns a piece of the operation and loves to play in his own games. "Hi Corky, wanna lay two hundred to a hundred? The point is 10."

"It's a bet, Ralph."

"Who else wants to lay a hundred to fifty? Carmine, you got it? Frankie, you okay?"

"Yeah Ralph, I'm okay," says Frankie.

"Hey, Frankie," says Corky, "after this shot let's go eat some chinks, okay?"

"Yeah," says Frankie. "I'm $700 in front. Whadya wanna do?

"If I win the next bet, its $1400. We'll pack up. $2100 buys a lot a chink food."

Corky and Frankie are getting up to leave and Ralph asks for everyone's attention. He has an announcement to make. "Listen everybody. I wanna get a message out. I got a piece of three joints. The last two nights my crew turned in eight G's of phony money. I better not find another buck that's phony in any of my games again 'cause when I catch the guy or guys, they won't like the payoff, I promise!"

Frankie and Corky leave the game and are driving downtown. Corky says, "Frankie, listen to this. I was in Mickey's Joint last night havin' a sandwich when Tommy Traino sits down. He says '*Come outside, I wanna show you somethin'.*" We go outside, he looks around and then opens the trunk of his car. Frankie, I almost fuckin' died. He had half a million bucks in the trunk. But guess what it was? Phony money! If he didn't tell me it was phony, there's no way you could tell. He had 20's, 50's, 100's – perfect! $18.00 per $100. I told him I'd let him know."

"Corky, just forget it. Are you nuts? That's the Feds – the F.B.I. – Secret Service. Those guys went to college. They know all the moves. Just forget the whole fuckin' thing. You gotta be nuts!"

"Listen Frankie, hear me out. We go to all three crap games. We bet Pres side up, (the phony money) against the Green side (the good money). Capeesh? We win the bet. Green side under bankroll. We always bet Pres 'til we run out. We can't miss, Frankie . . . anyway, we bought $10,000 worth."

"I swear to God, Corky, I think you got more crazy while I was away, but I like the idea even though I think you're gonna get us killed, and not by the cops."

"Aw c'mon, Frankie, how long you wanna live anyway? If we get caught, they can't call the cops, right? So we take a beatin'. We just wear heavy clothes. A beatin' don't hurt that much."

"Jesus Christ, you're nuts, Corky, you know it?"

....

Frankie kisses his mom and dad goodbye. Uncle Pete is driving him to the station after the farewell party. He has tears in his eyes and you can see in his face that he's thinking: *A seventeen year old kid goin' to Korea - this kid may never come back.*

It's a lousy feeling for Frankie, too. He hugs Uncle Pete, turns around and boards the train with a bunch of other G.I.'s. They are on their way to Pittsburg, California in the San Francisco Bay area where they will ship out to Korea.

On the train, Frankie gets bored. He has one dice on a key chain and another kid on the train has another dice. Frankie says, "Let's put the dice together and have a crap game." The dice are different colors – one red and one green – the funniest looking dice you've ever seen. They rob everybody on the train of their money.

....

Ten days after sailing out for Korea on the *Aiken Victory*, the ship's crew of Merchant Marines and 63rd Infantry Division Army personnel awake at dawn in the Pacific to find the sky dark and brooding, the sea choppy and the winds brisk. Throughout the morning, the ship's deck bows and dips, swinging in wide arcs across the horizon. By midafternoon, the barometer is falling steadily; the winds moan and heavy rains batter everyone on board.

"Hey Ralphie, this boat is sure rockin'. Some sailor said we're headin' into a typhoon or somethin'."

"Yeah Frankie, tell me about it. I've been seasick since we left port and I know you gotta be tired of holding me over the side of the ship."

"Ralphie, you keep throwin' up and you're gonna die. You're already so skinny I can't see ya when you turn sidewise."

"Okay wise-guy, but these typhoons are serious. I heard of ships sinkin' and guys bein' washed overboard."

As the days wear on, the violence of the wind increases. It shrieks and roars and the sea convulses. Typhoon Catherine is upon them and they are being pounded by violent gusts of wind and rain. Over and over, mountains of water rise up to engulf the ship.

Frankie is Corporal of the Guard and it's his job to go up on deck during the storm to make sure everyone is at their designated station. He clings desperately to the heavy ropes as he works his way around the ship.

He finds a Merchant Marine on watch in a lifeboat on the deck. The lifeboat is swaying violently back and forth.

"Man, I'm freezing! I'm so cold, I can't take it." Frankie asks, "What's your name, pal?" "Cherry," the Marine replies.

"You want some coffee, Cherry?"

"Yeah, please. I can't take this cold much longer."

"Okay, just hold on," Frankie tells him.

Frankie goes back along the ship, holding tight to the heavy ropes so he isn't washed overboard, all the way to the Galley to get this guy some coffee. He fills a cup, but by the time he gets back to where Cherry was, there's maybe an inch of coffee left in the cup. He looks in the lifeboat and hollers, "Hey Cherry, I got coffee." Cherry isn't there and Frankie assumes he got relieved and is probably down below sleeping. "Thank God, the poor guy sure needed some rest."

Next morning at Reveille, the storm has finally subsided and everyone comes up on deck with their duffle bags. All the men are lined up and there's these two duffle bags sitting there on the deck – unclaimed. Two guys washed over the side of the ship during the night. One of them was Cherry.

The storm lasts nine days and at the end of it, three G.I.'s and one sailor washed overboard. The ship has a broken fantail and after 23 days at sea limps into port at Yokohama Bay, Japan for repairs.

Frankie and Ralphie go up on deck and they see a houseboat docked right next to their ship. While they're standing there, Frankie hears a couple of guys on the houseboat talking and they're speaking in Italian. Frankie says, "Ralphie, where the hell are we, Italy?"

The 1st Lieutenant comes up on deck and says, "Do you Dago's hear those Italians talking?"

Frankie says, "Yes sir, me and Ralphie both speak Italian." He asks the Lieutenant, "sir, would you give us permission to visit them on board their houseboat?"

"Yeah, all right, but be back by chow time at 5pm."

"Thanks Lieutenant!"

Before they go, they've stolen some American cigarettes that they decide to sell to the Japanese that are hanging around the ship. They sell the cigarettes for 500 yen. From the side of the ship, they also sell stolen cans of chocolate syrup for 900 yen. They end up with a whole pile of Japanese yen.

Boarding the houseboat, Frankie and Ralphie meet the two Italian men who tell them that they have been docked there for a year. They are considered the enemy and cannot leave Yokohama Bay for four more years under some obscure International Law. They mention "President Street" in Brooklyn which is known for having a number of notorious mobsters living next door to each other. And it just so happens that Ralphie is from Presidents Street.

One of the Italians says that he has a cousin in Brooklyn and Ralphie asks, "What's your cousin's name?"

The man says, "Joe Farina" and he goes below deck and comes back up with a photo of his cousin from Brooklyn.

Well, Ralphie can't believe it. He recognizes the name and the photo as that of his second cousin. That makes Ralphie and this Italian guy related! Imagine, meeting an Italian guy from Italy on a houseboat in Japan who has a cousin in Brooklyn who turns out to be your cousin too! After hugging and kissing, Frankie tells Ralphie, "Let's make our *paisano's* rich," so they give them all of the Japanese currency that they have, and the Italian guys consider them their heroes. Later, Frankie and Ralphie learn that the Japanese yen is worthless in Korea anyway.

A few days later, the *Aiken Victory* leaves Yokohama Bay for Korea. Korea has been under Japanese occupation since 1910 and as late as early 1947 the Korean peninsula is still occupied by a few Japanese. Frankie and the 63rd Infantry Division are to keep the peace and help liberate the Korean people from the remaining Japanese.

Landing at Yong Dung Po Harbor off the Yellow Sea, the temperatures are 10-12 degrees colder, hovering around zero. Frankie tells Ralphie, "I don't see no warm beaches or hot Korean girls in sarongs like they told us in

Basic, do you Ralphie?"

Ralphie says, "No and I don't know about you, Frankie, but I'm feelin' kinda sick since Chow."

"Yeah Ralphie, I don't feel so good either."

Turns out somebody put laundry soap in the big vat of soup on the mess deck. It's just before New Year's with zero degree temperatures and guys are wearing everything that's been issued to them to try to keep warm, and you got 1400 guys with dysentery and they're vomiting all over the place. They have to peel off all their clothes to take a shit and then have to put everything back on again. The frozen ground is hard as a rock so they can't dig holes to bury their feces. The place stinks, its freezing cold and everybody's wet, dirty and miserable. First Lieutenant Scott says, "You see that light way off in the distance? Well, that's where we're gonna get the railroad car to transport us to camp." They start walking.

Frankie says to Ralphie, "Look at that light. A railroad car will be a hellava lot better than bein' out in the open and freezin' to death." They walk for a while.

"Frankie, just leave me here. I can't take this. I wanna die."

"Stop bein' so stupid! Come with me."

"I can't make it, Frankie."

"Just gimme your duffle bag," says Frankie.

Frankie carries both his and Ralphie's duffle bags and Ralphie is hanging on to Frankie's arm. They slip on the icy ground. They fall and get up, fall and get up again all the way up one hill and down, and up another hill and down again. Ralphie keeps saying, "Just leave me on the ground, I can't make it."

"Just hang on, buddy." Frankie keeps telling him.

When they finally make it to where the railroad cars are, Frankie collapses on the ground, so tired that his legs give out. After about 15 minutes, he's able to get up and get on the railroad car which consists of four wheels and a bombed-out flatbed with no roof or walls. Everybody is wearing everything they own and they're still freezing. Some Korean kids appear out of nowhere dressed in nothing but shirts with no shoes on their feet. The bottoms of their feet have calluses an inch thick and they walk right on the frozen rails in their bare feet. They beg for cigarettes. Frankie tells Ralphie, "Look at these fuckin' kids, they got no shirts on and we're sittin' here all bundled up and freezin' like a bastard." Frankie and Ralphie give them whatever they have as do most of the other G.I.'s.

The men are jammed into Army trucks to take them to camp Hillameyer. Colonel Hillameyer was killed and the camp was named after him. All the streets in the camp are named after G.I.'s that have been killed.

The Koreans live in mud huts that have fires underneath to keep them warm. At night, you can see the lights from the hut fires as well as the lights from the lanterns that they carry. It's eerie and foreign and everybody's scared.

Frankie is just being Frankie and can't seem to stay out of trouble. He's been thrown out of three company's and has earned the reputation of having an arrogant wise-guy attitude. He refuses KP duty and that night Staff Sergeant Boner, a fifteen year Army veteran from North Dakota, assigns a post to each guy in the Platoon. Sgt. Boner is a lanky guy, balding with a big nose, bad teeth and skin as white as milk.

The guys all get on the truck and it's dark and cold with torrential rains. A kid named Billy is driving and he says, "Okay Wilson, this is your Perimeter Post, get out." They go another few miles and another guy is given a post and he gets out. Finally, Frankie is the last of the G.I.'s left on the truck and they are leaving the camp, going outside the camp gate. Frankie says, "Hey, where am I goin'?"

"Don't worry about it soldier, we're gonna take care of you."

A few miles outside the camp is a huge 40 ton rock crusher just sitting there in the middle of nowhere. It's pouring down rain. The driver says, "This is your post, Soldier."

"Where? Where's my post and what am I guarding?" asks Frankie.

"You're gonna guard that rock crusher."

"We're not even in camp! We're outside the camp!" says Frankie.

"That's what you get tough guy."

The watch is eight hours in the rain and the dark with freezing temperatures. Frankie has his M1 rifle and the driver tells him, "Get under the machine. Do whatever you want, but this is your Post and you're to be here and remember that you're protecting this rock crusher. If anybody comes around, you shoot 'em."

"I'm not gonna shoot nobody for a rock crusher. Who the hell would want this old rusted out piece'a shit equipment? Whaydya think, the gooks are gonna carry it away? What am I supposed to protect here?"

"I know you. You're one of those smart ass New York guys. I know your kind." He laughs and drives away.

Frankie gets under the wheel of the rock crusher to keep out of the rain and holding his M1 rifle he is thinking, "What the fuck am I doin' here? I grew up in New York stealin' stuff and look what I got myself into here. I swear to God, when I get home I'm gonna kill this Sgt. Boner!" He's really scared and Frankie doesn't scare easily. But when you're 17 years old in a foreign country and its freezing cold, dark and pouring down rain and you're 5 miles outside the camp, alone, underneath some big ass rock crusher in the middle of a rice paddy field and all you hear is the sound of howling and all you can see are little white lights in the fog off in the distance, man, you're scared. After a long while, Frankie finally falls into a fitful half-asleep.

Suddenly, he sees two bright lights coming towards him. He says to himself, "Okay, my job is to guard this rock crusher," so he jumps up and pointing his rifle yells, "Halt or I'll shoot," he knows full well that it's the army truck coming to pick him up, but wanting to show that he's on the job. The driver says, "Ah, put that fuckin' gun down and get in the truck!"

When they get back to the barracks, Frankie falls on his cot and is out cold. All of a sudden, he wakes up on the floor and thinks he's dreaming. Staff Sgt. Boner is standing over him after lifting the cot up and throwing Frankie to the floor. He says, "Hey Soldier, you didn't put your mosquito netting on!" Half asleep, Frankie jumps up and punches the Sergeant in the nose.

The next morning at Reveille, Sgt. Boner isn't smiling. Before dismissing the Platoon, he says, "Somebody had a lesson about mosquito nets last night. Does anyone have anything to say about that?" Frankie steps out and says, "Take off that striped shirt and I'll knock the shit outta ya right here in front of this whole fuckin' Platoon."

Told to pack up his gear and report to the Company Commander, Frankie finds himself once again in front of Capt. Smith. "What Army do you think you're in, Private? You're the worst soldier I've ever seen. I should bring you up on charges and give you a BCD. I should'a given you a BCD back in Basic at Ft. Jackson. What do you have to say about that, Private?"

"Captain, you're a fair man, sir. What would you do after bein' at a post five miles outside camp for eight hours in the cold and rain and then get back to barracks and get tossed off your cot when you're in a dead sleep? I'm sorry to be a bother to you again, sir, but please give me one more chance. I promise I won't cause you no more trouble, sir."

The Captain looks at Frankie and shakes his head with half a smile on his face. "You're a piss poor soldier, but I'm not gonna throw you out 'cause you're a personable kind'a guy. I'm shipping you out of Company K and assigning you to the Airplane Hanger with the gooks and you're gonna clean it out and make it a Recreation Hall. You're to report to Corporal Woods. Now get outta here. I never wanna see you again. Dismissed."

The Army can't figure out anything else to do with Frankie.

....

Corporal Woods stops by the hangar. "They sent you here, huh?"

Frankie says, "Yeah, I guess so, sir." "Well, whadya gonna do here?"

"I don't know," says Frankie. "They said somethin' about makin' it a Rec Hall."

"Well, you and these gooks need to get all this stuff cleaned up – pick-up the beer and soda cans and get rid of all the garbage. And you better earn Korean 'cause you're gonna be livin' with these gooks and these are your new quarters. Any questions?"

"What, you gotta be kiddin'," says Frankie. "I'm gonna pick up all this garbage?"

"Look, in another two weeks I'm goin' home so they'll probably leave you here with the gooks."

Frankie says, "All right, but what's gonna happen to me?" "Maybe they'll put you in charge here," says the Corporal.

Frankie's thinking that maybe that wouldn't be so bad. He gets the Korean guys to pick-up all the garbage and clean-out the hangar and names the place the "Chingo Club". There are eight Koreans assigned to him and Frankie makes friends with all of them. They like him and in no time at all he's got them doing his bidding and stealing stuff for him. A couple of guys build him a private bedroom with doors in a corner of the Hall and he's living like a King. Honey is a fag Korean kid who says, "I take care of Frankie san." Honey becomes Frankie's personal valet. Another guy that Frankie calls "Yo Yo" warns him whenever the top brass are coming.

....

Captain Joe Campana is the doctor in charge of the Medical Company. He was drafted and he tells Frankie, "I gotta get outta this Army!" They're riding in a truck and the Captain tells him, "Hey, you wear my hat with the Captain bars and I'll wear your Private's hat. Don't forget you gotta salute when anybody comes by." He says, "Frankie let's get some broads."

There's like a million Korean girls all wanting to get in the truck with Frankie yelling, "Oh G.I., oh G.I."

They're starving to death and will go anywhere and do anything for whatever the soldiers give them: candy, apples, whatever they have. The Captain says,

"Let's sneak 'em back to camp. I'll test 'em and the ones that are clean, we'll have 'em take showers."
They get back to camp and the doc finishes the tests.

They have a jump and then they put each girl that tested clean in a separate barracks and forty guys jump her for whatever they've got to give to her.

....

Corporal Woods ships out for home and Captain Smith pays Frankie a visit at the Rec Hall. He says, "Listen up soldier, I'm making you a Corporal."

Frankie says, "I don't wanna be a Corporal, sir."

"Look, you have to be a Corporal because you're the only G.I. here and somebody has to be in charge of the Rec Hall and the Koreans that are here." He turns to get in his Jeep saying, "So long Corporal."

Frankie is assigned a Jeep and it's his job to take the garbage (cigarette butts, trash, food scraps, whatever the G.I.'s throw away) to the garbage pit. He backs the Jeep up to the pit and is instantly surrounded by Koreans who jump into the pit. Kids step on old people, pushing them aside. It's survival of the fittest. The strong take butt cans and scrape up the garbage, eating it raw. Frankie makes the trip to the pit three times. The fourth time, he takes his rifle and shoots it into the air out of desperation. He finds himself crying on the way back to the Rec Hall. After that, he assigns a Private to do the garbage runs twice a week.

Summer comes and it's so hot you can smell the gooks from a mile away. The Koreans make a dish called "Kimchee" which consists of cabbage pickled in a solution of garlic, salt and red chili peppers. They bury it in the ground and it ferments and everything for miles around smells like a garbage dump. The gooks stink like Billy Goats.

Inside the Rec Hall, Frankie and his guys make cookies and donuts for the G.I.'s. There are packaged cookies leftover from 1942-43 that have bugs and rat droppings in them and Frankie puts those out too. The G.I.'s come to socialize, laugh, drink beer and soda, and eat.

The 1st Lieutenant is a young guy about 22. He is tall, skinny, wears glasses and looks like a mama's boy just out of college. He comes out to inspect the hangar and Yo Yo warns Frankie that he's coming.

Inside the Rec Hall is a long counter with a conveyer belt and a big vat of hot oil at one end, and this is where Frankie and his guys make the cookies and the donuts. Frankie hears the Lieutenant's Jeep pull up and takes off his shirt. He's sweating like a pig and leaning over the counter with sweat dripping off him when the Lieutenant comes into the Hall. Frankie hears, "Ten Hut". The Lieutenant says, "Where's your shirt, soldier?"

"It's hotter 'n hell, sir."

The Lieutenant says, "What are you doing there?"

Frankie says, "I'm makin' these cookies, sir."

The Lieutenant is watching Frankie as he picks up the cookie dough and slaps it against his sweaty belly to make an indentation in the cookie with his belly button.

"What are you doing there, soldier?"

"Nothin', just makin' these cookies, sir," says Frankie. "They look better with this little hole in 'em."

"Are you crazy?"

"Lieutenant, you think it's bad doin' this? What? Is it against the Health rules or somethin'?"

He says, "Of course it's against the Health Code, you idiot!"

116

Frankie says, "You should see when I make the donuts."

The Lieutenant says, "I gotta get out of here! You are crazy!" He turns and runs out of the hangar. It is his job to come out to inspect the place every week, but after that incident Frankie never sees him again.

....

The *Chingo Club* has a Korean All-Girl Revue to entertain the G.I.'s. Jackie is a volunteer Social Worker from the U.S. attached to the USO and stationed at Camp Hillameyer. She works with Frankie to help supervise the shows. Jackie is about 29, a pretty redhead, but a little on the chubby side. Frankie doesn't care – he's 18.

In his makeshift bedroom in the Rec Hall, Frankie has a pot belly stove. Its Army rules that all fires are to be out by 10 PM. Jackie is staying the night and Frankie has kept the fire burning in the stove. Seeing smoke coming from the Rec Hall, the Provost Marshal breaks in and finds Frankie in bed with Jackie.

"Well, well, lookie here. We're finally catching you in the act, Corporal. Your arrogant attitude has caught up with you this time: Cohabitating with a female on Army property, fires burning after 10 PM. These are grounds for a Court Martial and Dishonorable Discharge. You're lookin' at prison time, soldier."

Frankie starts to stutter, this time at a loss for words. Jackie gets up from the cot and says, "Wait a minute."

"This has nothing to do with you, young lady."

"I really wish you would reconsider, sir. I would hate to have to notify my father."

"And just who is your father, young lady?"

Jackie says, "My father is General Devoe."

The Provost Marshal is stunned by this revelation and after a long pause says, "Well, I really didn't see a fire and you were just visiting, so there's no problem here. I'm sorry for the inconvenience." He turns and walks out.

....

The Koreans have beautiful embroidered fabric. It is against Military Law to ship anything home from the army while in Military service, but since Jackie is a volunteer, Frankie uses her name to send 40 yards of fabric home. Frankie's mom makes draperies for all of the windows in the house.

....

Vikki is a Red Cross worker. Frankie is saying, "I'm tellin' you, Vikki, I'm crazy about you."

"Yeah right, Frankie. There's only three women in camp. You've been in Korea too long. Besides, I'm twice your age. Why don't you follow the rules and behave yourself? The Captain's wife, Kathy, told me that the Captain wants to have you Court Martialed for selling food and G.I. clothes to the Koreans. She also said some other things. You're lucky she likes you. And, boy does she like you, you bastard!"

"Yeah, yeah, I can't wait to get back to New York where I can make some big money instead of this penny ante shit. In Korea, the only way to make big money is opium and I hate that shit. I hate dope. That's not for me, ya know what I mean, Vikki?"

Frankie's ship anchors at Puget Sound, WA after 13 days at sea. Everybody who was on board is looking for a telephone. Frankie is in a phone booth. "C'mon Operator, try again. I just got back from Korea. . . yeah, I'll wait, but hurry up, okay? . . . hello, hello, Mom, I'm home! No, I'm in Washington, Ma. I love you all! How's Dad and Gramma and Uncle Pete and Joey and Petey? Man, it's good to hear you, Mom! Yeah, make some macaroni and gravy! I'm dyin' for some of your cookin'! Yeah, I feel good, Ma. *Madone*, I sure miss America! I'll be home in three days. . . 'Cause I gotta go through processing and discharge. You seen Corky, Mom? I hope he's not in jail." Frankie laughs. "I learned a lot of things here, Mom. Everything is gonna be great from now on . . . I'm sorry, Ma, I gotta go. Lots of guys wanna call home too. I love you! I'll call you tomorrow. Bye."

CHAPTER FIVE

The family has moved from the apartment over the grocery store to a small house.

"What a beautiful house, Ma. Everybody looks great. Oh man, that smell – gravy and meatballs! I used to dream about it, especially on Sundays."

"Sonny, you look like Tarzan," says Uncle Pete. "Look at that build! You should be in the movies."

Connie says, "Pete, you're gonna give him a big head. C'mon, sit down and let's eat. Sonny, here's your mac, meatballs, sausage and a piece of pork – your favorites."

"C'mon, eat'a some salad first," says Gramma. "I make'a some bread just for you, Sonny. Here, have some wine, *coma bella figlya*."

"I can't believe I'm home! What a beautiful house, great food and a great family!"

Joe asks, "You got any plans, Son, about what you're gonna do? I don't mean today or tomorrow . . . but in the future."

"Yeah, I got plans, Dad."

Connie says, "Well, Sonny, you know Dad's got the fish market now and he needs a partner to help him and Uncle Pete. That's all he keeps talkin' about."

"That's out, Ma. Joey and Petey can keep helpin' out at the store." The boys groan. "I'm not gonna break my back the way I did when I was a kid. I've got other things on my mind."

"Now don't start talkin' nonsense," says Connie. "You were in serious trouble before you went in the army."

"Take it easy, babe," says Joe. "He just got home. C'mon, the food's getting' cold."

"Have'a some wine," says Gramma. "Good for the stomach. It kills the worms."

....

Mickey's Joint is the neighborhood Italian restaurant. It seats fifty people and has a separate bar with a photo wall of all the Italian greats: Sinatra, Damone, Bennett, Frank Costello, Luciano, and a few others with no names. Corky and Frankie are sitting in a booth in the far corner. Corky says, "You remember Big Frank, THE boss in Brooklyn? I did some work for him through one of his guys. He said he liked me and when a spot opened he'd send for me."

"Corky, how the hell did you meet him? He runs half of Brooklyn, all the docks and he's got the Longshoremen's Union. What the hell did you do?"

"Take it easy, Frankie. Rico was in *Sing Sing* with him and he does a lot of work for Big Frank. He needed another guy for some heavy stuff, Rico gave me a shot and it came out perfect. Since then, whenever they don't use the Brooklyn guys, they call Rico, he calls me and we make the score or whatever, capeesh?"

"Corky, I'm proud of you. If you go with him, tell him I'm interested, okay?"

"I was gonna do that anyway, Frankie."

....

Big Frank is a "made guy". His rank is Captain and he's in control of everything - his word is law. He is in need of some good people after having recently lost a couple of guys – one guy is doing ten years in the joint and the other just disappeared. Frankie and Corky are meeting with him at the *Hollis Diner* in Elmhurst. Whenever Big Frank has a meeting, the owner, Bill, puts up a sign that reads: *"Closed for the Holiday"*. Makes no difference what day it is, when Big Frank is there the place is closed for the Holiday. The next day, the meeting is over and it's business as usual.

Corky says, "Big Frank, I'd like you to meet my *paisano*, Frankie 'Sonny' Basilio. I put my life on the line and vouch for him."

Big Frank says, "You come with strong juice, Frankie. Welcome. Have a hamburger and a cup a coffee."

Frankie is nervous, but he looks calm as a cucumber. "It's an honor to meet ya."

"Frankie, I want you to hang with me for two weeks and learn the ropes." Big Frank turns to Corky and says, "Looks like we might have a good man here."

A few weeks later, Frankie is introduced to "Mike the Spike". Mike is a large, ugly guy about 45 years old and Frankie can tell that he's not crazy about him. He guesses that Mike sees him as a young kid who doesn't know anything. Mike has buried more than a few bodies. He and Frankie are to grab the Jew Shylock on Broadway where he has a swanky office. The "outside" guy says that the Shylock has pockets sewn into his underwear where he keeps anywhere from $500 to $1,000 when he goes to see a client.

Mike's plan is to watch for him to come out of his office, pull up to the curb, grab him and put him in the car. Now the "Shy" is a heavy set Jew guy and Frankie realizes that he might yell or create a scene. They are meeting at the *Hollis Diner* and Frankie stands up and says, "Mike, lemme grab him and shove my pistol in his ribs and walk him to the car. Broadway is a very busy street."

Mike gets up and says, "You young fuck! Are you sayin' I'm afraid to use a pistol?" With that, he pulls out a gun and sticks it in Frankie's neck.

Big Frank says, "Put that fuckin' gun away, Mike. He's with me, you stupid bastard."

Mike looks at Frankie and says, "I got nine guys under my belt. You better be glad you're with Big Frank or you'd be number ten."

Frankie realizes that he just about made the biggest mistake of his life – one that could have ended it right then and there.

....

Frankie and Corky are at Hollywood Al's Clothing Store in Harlem. Buster, a black guy, owns the place and is a friend. The customers in the store are all sharp dressers. They wear high-waist pants with peg legs and have ducktail haircuts. This is where the "Gee's" (the grifters and con men) buy their clothes.

Frankie and Corky are looking around at the merchandise when a salesman walks over. "Hello, I'm Henry. We've got some new material from England. Want to take a look?"

Corky says, "Go tell Buster that Corky and Frankie are here and wanna see him."

"Sure, no problem, I'll go look in the back for him."

After a few moments, Buster enters from the back. "Hey Frankie, Corky, how you doin'? Wanna come in the back and have a drink?"

"No thanks," says Frankie. "That guy Henry said you got some material from England. Let's have a look at it."

Corky asks, "Buster, you got any material from Italy?" He shakes his head and Corky looks at

Frankie, "I think Buster is prejudiced, Frankie." They all laugh.

Buster shows them a beautiful bolt of cloth and Frankie says, "Corky, let's get four or five suits each, okay?" Corky nods and begins to explain to Buster what he wants.

"You guys haven't put on any weight since the last time. I got your measurements: 26 knee, 15 peg and draped jacket 1 inch below fingertip, right?"

Corky tells him, "You're a genius, Buster. You should open up another store, you'd be a millionaire."

Buster is writing up a sales slip and Frankie says, "Take it easy with that pen, pal. Make me a deal and I'll make you a better one."

Looking at Frankie, Corky says, "Sometimes I think you're a Jew. Tell him to throw in a coupl'a hats."

Buster says, "I took 20% off the bill, fellas. You owe me $800."

"Okay Buster, here's my deal," says Frankie. "I'll give you $300 cash and $700 credit in numbers and horses. You might get lucky and beat our brains out. Everybody else is, eh Corky? Besides, you make an extra $200."

Corky says, "We got hit three times this week. 811-406-625 for three G's and the week ain't over yet."

"Man, you guys run a hard bargain, but it's a deal. You may just buy me that other store."

"You're a sharp cat, Buster," says Corky. "See you in two weeks."

....

Frankie has been home from the army for a couple of years and he's involved in a lot of different things – a little of this – a little of that. The newest enterprise is stealing cars. The operation has been set up by the upper echelon. Frankie's old friend, Eddie Lab, is involved and he's set up a crew of guys that include Frankie. It works like this: somebody steals a new prestige car – a Cadillac, Lincoln, Mercedes, etc. Regular transports of luxury cars are scheduled for shipment overseas from the docks to different parts of the world. They take the Vin numbers off the cars scheduled for shipment and put them on the new stolen cars. The cars that the Vin numbers have been taken from are shipped out. They have an inside guy at the DMV in Providence, RI and he registers the stolen cars with the new Vin numbers. Then the cars are sold and the buyers get a legitimate registration. It's fool proof.

Corky and Frankie buy a 1951 Olds – Green and Black. Four months later they lose it in a crap game. They run out of money so they put up the car registration and lose it.

The car operation goes on for quite a while and everybody is making good money. One day, they sell a car to a guy and he's driving down 2nd Avenue and hears a siren. A cop pulls him over and he says, "Uh, uh Officer, I didn't do nothin' wrong!"

The cop asks, "Why are you so nervous, sir?"

"Look, I don't know nothin. I had nothing to do with this!" "You had nothing to do with what?" asks the Officer.

"Well you know, you probably looked up the car and know that it's stolen. I just bought it from a guy."

The cop takes him downtown, he's interrogated and gives up everything. The car is impounded. They lift the hood and do an acid/lye test to get the original numbers off the motor. The guy ends up in jail, loses the car and the whole operation is busted.

....

Big Frank runs the docks at Bush Terminal. Stuff comes into the docks and Frankie and Corky back up their truck, load it up and take off. The guy that checks the trucks out as they are leaving the terminal is their man too. It's a big syndicate of people.

Frankie and Corky get back to the neighborhood with grosses of shirts in boxes. All the shirts are red and green. They sell every shirt and the next day everybody in the neighborhood is running around with red and green shirts on. Whatever Frankie and Corky sell, you see everybody in the neighborhood wearing that same thing. One week it's shirts, the next week it's hats, then pants. And everybody is walking around in the same stuff. It's a riot. They sell suits for $100 that sell for $500 in the stores.

CHAPTER SIX

It is early morning and behind a large tank filled with slithering eels, Joe and his brother Pete sit drinking coffee. At the left side of the store in a long glass case, fresh fish are displayed over ice. The heads and tails are still intact. Bunches of fresh parsley stick out here and there from between the sunfish, cod, perch, mackerel and clams. The different varieties of fish are separated on trays and divided by streamers of brightly colored plastic ribbon in red, white and green - the colors of the Italian flag.

At the end of the fish case, a young good-looking guy stands lifting weights in front of a mirror. Papa Joe and Uncle Pete stare at him. Papa Joe says, "Joey, you're always liftin' those weights. Don't you get tired? You already look like Tarzan with those muscles. Besides, this is a fish store, not the gym and it's time to open.

"Papa, I'm gonna win Mr. America, and pretty soon the store will be full of pretty girls come to watch me." He laughs as he goes to the front door, unlocks the lock and flips the sign over to read "OPEN". Then he gives a weather report as he goes back to the center counter to fold aprons and start cleaning fish.

"Boy, the sun is hotter than an oven already."

Papa Joe says, "Joey, don't worry about the pretty girls and the weather! You need to make sure the ice don't melt on the fish. They're getting' old already."

Sol the Tailor with the shop next door pops his head in and Papa Joe and Pete tell him, "C'mon in Sol. Have a cup a coffee. We just made some fresh."

Sol is tall and thin with a thick mop of salt and pepper hair and bushy eyebrows. He has deep-set eyes that are dark and sad. His nose is big and he rarely smiles. *"What's to smile about?"* he's always saying.

Joey is cleaning fish as the telephone rings. Papa Joe gets up from the table to answer it. Seeing that papa has answered the phone, Joey goes to the bathroom.

"Hello, fish market . . . yeah, this is Mr. Basilio." There's a long pause while Papa Joe listens intently. The expression on his face changes to pain and anger. "You're gonna expel my son, Petey, from school? How can you do that? He's a good boy. We want him to finish school, Mrs. . . . Mrs. . . . What's your name again?" He listens for another short pause and then yells into the phone, "Well, we're gonna just see about that, Mrs. Sower . . . Mrs. Sower?? . . . That's a good name for you, you sower. . ." He slams the phone down.

Pete and Sol are staring at him and Pete says, "Joe what's goin' on? What's the matter?" "Who's this Mrs. Sower?" asks Sol.

Joey comes out of the bathroom and hearing the raised voices, asks,

"What's goin' on? What about Mrs. Sower? Tell me so I can break her head!"

"I'm okay, Joey. Go on now and clean the fish. I'll tell you later, not now." Joey goes back to cleaning the fish.

Sol is biting nervously on his lip and pours some fresh coffee. Pete watches Joe's eyes fill with tears. His face is flushed red and he's mad as hell. Sol and Pete try to console him.

Sol says, "Raise kids, Joe, you see what happens? Come on, relax, drink your coffee."

Pete is pacing back and forth, getting angrier by the minute seeing his brother so upset. "I'm sorry, I gotta get outta here for a while. I'll be back later." And he leaves the store.

Papa Joe continues, "Kids! They give you a lot a heartaches, Sol. I try to raise 'em right, but they just don't listen. I'm failing, Sol."

"Joe, you gotta stop blaming yourself. The kids today are wild. Just pick up the newspaper, you'll see what I mean."

"Petey's mama worries so much about him. She always says, '*If he doesn't get an education, how will he make a living?*' You know, Petey's not like Frankie and Joey. They're hustlers, they'll always make a buck. But Petey, his heart's too big. All that stuff he collects in his room, he gives it away to his friends. Imagine, they elected him President of his class – not for his grades but just because they *love* him." Papa Joe chokes up when he says that and Sol nods his head in sympathy.

"Joe, you gotta understand. Education is a great thing, yes, and college too, but not everybody can do it. You know what I mean?"

"What could he do without an education?"
"Well," . . . Sol pauses.

"I'm waiting, Sol."

Sean McGuire, the neighborhood beat cop, enters the store. He's your typical smiling Irishman, a big strapping guy over 6 feet tall and weighing an easy 210 pounds.

"Hey Sean, I got a question for ya," says Joe. "Name me one good job you can get without an education."

"Joe, I didn't come for a job. I came to pick up my package of fish."

Sol says, "I got it, Joe! - a carpenter, a brick layer, a truck driver." "Oh no Sol, that's no good, it's too much like hard work for Petey."

Joey comes out from the back of the store and spots the cop, Sean McGuire. "Hey, it must be Friday, here's Big Sean. How you doin'?" Joey goes over to him, shakes his hand while looking him up and down and gives a little laugh.

"Well Tarzan, I'm ready for you! This time I'm gonna get you good!" Joey says, "Okay, let's go!"

The two men go over to the counter and lean down in an arm wrestling position. Sean calls time out long enough to open his jacket then they lock arms and nothing gives either way. Sean's eyes are set with determination and it's obvious how much he wants this win. He has never beaten Joey. Both men keep straining and holding steady with nothing giving until suddenly there is a ripping noise. Sean's jacket is tearing at the back seam. At that moment, Joey puts Sean's arm down and the struggle is over. Joey gives him a friendly laugh, but Sean's face is red as a lobster. He's not happy that he lost again.

Papa Joe says, "You guys act like kids."

As Sean gets up, Sol says to him, "You ripped your jacket. Come next door with me and I'll mend it for you."

Sean and Sol are leaving the store and Joey comes around the counter with the package of fish. He gives Sean another friendly laugh.

"Yeah, yeah, laugh all you want, Joey. I'll get you next time so don't get too cocky."

Sean and Sol leave the Fish Store to go to Sol's Tailor Shop and Joey goes back behind the counter to continue cleaning the fish.

Papa Joe sees Frankie coming toward the store from the street. "Joey, here comes your brother. Now you listen and I'll tell you both about that Mrs. Sower."

Frankie enters the market and goes straight to Papa Joe and gives him a big hug. Looking hard at him, he can see that something's wrong. "You're upset today, Papa. What's upsetting you?"

"They're gonna throw Petey outta school! The Principal, Mrs. Sower, called. She says he's nothin' but a juvenile delinquent. They can't do that, can they Frankie?"

"I don't know, Papa, but take it easy, all right? I'll handle this thing. I know this Mrs. Sower. She was the principal when I was at that school. I'll take care of it right now. Just don't get upset."

"Mrs. Sower. What a name, huh? She's gonna give me a heart attack."

"No papa, we're gonna give her one. Hey, Joey, take Papa home then come back and watch the store, will ya? I'll go straighten this thing out with Petey and this Sower broad."

....

Driving down Grand Central Parkway on the way to *PS 14,* Frankie spots a flower shop and has an idea. He goes into the shop and comes back out with a dozen long stemmed red roses.

At the school, he parks his Cadillac, enters the school building and locates the principal's office. He knocks on the office door and a tall, attractive redhead in her mid-40's answers, saying, "Come in, come in Mr. Basilio. I've been expecting you. I remember you and I want you to know that I am not intimidated by your kind. What I say goes around here, I hope you understand. I have the authority. Where is your father anyway?"

Frankie sets the vase with the dozen red roses in the middle of Mrs. Sower's desk. "Couldn't we call a truce?"

"Get those flowers off my desk! You can't bribe me that way! Please, get them off this desk!! This is solid cherry mahogany – a family heirloom. But what would you know about heirlooms!? Look! You've stained it! Get them off this desk at once!"

"Take them off yourself lady. Tell me, what did my brother do?"

With her hands trembling, she puts the flowers on the floor and frantically rubs the top of her desk with a soft towel, mumbling under her breath, *"I'll be glad to get rid of your kind."*

She continues saying, "Look Mr. Basilio, your brother talks in class and is disruptive. I caught him smoking in the back room. He's had three warnings. That's it. Anyway, well, he's not really college material, you know? It's a disgrace that they elected him President of his class."

"No lady, you're the disgrace. Ever think of working in a prison?" He gets up to leave. "Thanks for nothin'." Frankie walks out of the principal's office, goes to his car and drives back to the fish market where Joey and Petey are sitting and talking.

Petey has his dog with him. He's a mixed breed with long shaggy hair. Petey is 16 years old. He's wearing green peg pants with yellow pastel pockets. He's a real jokester, has the charisma of a movie star and a great sense of humor. You can't get mad at him, and he keeps Papa Joe shaking his head, saying, "*Is this my kid?*"

Petey is saying, "I'm telling you, the teacher hates me. She says my IQ is 'only average' and that I'll never be nothin' but a delinquent. To tell the truth, I know I'm no Einstein. I hate math. Nobody likes Math, do they?"

"I may just have'ta visit this bitch," says Joey.

"Petey, she says you never pay attention, you talk in class and she caught you smokin' in the back room. She warned you, is that true or not?" asks Frankie.

"Yeah, it's true. I hate that school and I hate that Mrs. Sower!"

Frankie tells him, "You don't have to go to that school no more, Petey. And you don't have to see Mrs. Sower-face. We'll get you in a Vocational School and you can learn a trade. You just meet me here in the morning at 9:00 AM sharp, okay? We'll get your records from that Mrs. Sower."

Changing the subject, Frankie turns to Joey and says, "Joey, you know anybody that's got a chain saw?

Yeah, you heard me, a chain saw. I'm gonna need it tonight. Don't forget. I got my reasons, okay? And keep your mouth shut."

"Yeah," says Joey, "and George Washington had his reasons too when he cut down his father's tree. I'll get it for ya, don't worry, Frankie."

Getting up to leave, Frankie says, "You guys get to work and sell some fish, will ya!"

....

The next morning, the boys give Papa Joe the day off. Joey opens the store, checks the weather, looks at himself in the mirror, flexes his muscles and smiles. Sol the Tailor enters.

"Good Morning, Joey. Where's Papa Joe?"

"He took the day off Sol and today I'm in charge. I'm the boss." "Yeah right, Joey, you're the boss." He laughs. "With you Joey it's girls, girls and more girls. That's all you do, lift weights and chase girls."

"Sol, you're too serious. Go have some fun. Cheat on your wife. Get drunk. Buy some wild clothes." He laughs.

"I'm leaving. I'm glad I don't have any sons. I feel bad for your good father and mother. Joey, were you adopted? I wouldn't be surprised." He walks out, slamming the door behind him.

Petey arrives at the Fish Store and Joey says, "Well, well, here's the zoot suiter. I hope you're here to help."

"Frankie called and wants me to go with him to my school tomorrow instead of today. I don't get it. It's only down the street."

"So go tomorrow. I'm sure he has his reasons. C'mon, Petey, start cleanin' up the floor, will ya?"

"Okay," says Petey . . . "catch this" . . . and he throws a flounder at Joey. Joey picks up a mackerel and throws it at Petey. That starts the fish war with both boys yelling and laughing and throwing fish all over the store.

Mrs. Goldstein, a neighborhood lady, enters and almost gets hit in the head with a flying fish. She screams, "Are you boys crazy? Stop this immediately. Where is Papa Joe?"

"Oh hi Mrs. Goldstein," Petey says as he's putting down a fish.

"Joey's just practicing his pitching arm." Joey doubles over laughing. "See the fish, It's so fresh it just jumps right off the fish counter." Both boys are laughing hysterically.

"I came to pick-up my flounder. Your father promised me a fresh flounder!" She looks at the fish in the case, walks back and forth, eyeing the mackerel too. She spots the salmon. "How much does that salmon weigh? Maybe I'll take some of that too."

Joey brings the salmon out of the case and weighs it. "It weighs eight pounds, Mrs. Goldstein. That's a lot of fish."

"I'll take half of it. Four pounds is more than enough."

Joey takes the cleaver and abruptly cuts the fish in half, wraps it up and gives it to Mrs. Goldstein. "Here's your fish, Mrs. Goldstein."

She leaves the store in a huff, slamming the door behind her.

Joey goes behind the counter where he cut the salmon. He looks at the fish head with the fish eyes looking up at him. He looks over at Petey and he can't resist. "Hey, Petey catch this!" Joey throws the salmon head at Petey and hits him between the eyes.

The fish falls to the floor. Petey picks it up and throws it back, just missing Joey. Joey starts laughing and runs from behind the counter. He grabs some squid and throws it. Fish heads and tails are flying through the air. This is the scene as Mrs. Goldstein comes back into the store, flying fish tails barely missing her head. Screaming, she yells, "I forgot my flounder. My God! What's going on here?"

Joey and Petey both try to make excuses. Petey starts sweeping up the fish heads and tails and Joey tries to pacify Mrs. Goldstein. "We're sorry, Mrs. Goldstein, we got a little carried away. Please, let me get your package of flounder. I'll give you an extra pound for any trouble we caused you." He hurries back to the fish counter, but by now the smell of fish that isn't so fresh anymore is overwhelming and Mrs. Goldstein gets a whiff. She holds her forehead as if she is about to faint from the odor. "Oh God, never mind, just let me out of here, now!" She turns and hurries out of the store.

Petey says, "Frankie is coming by any minute. He'll kill us. Look at this mess!"

"When he comes in, I'll talk to him and you put this fish in his pocket. We might as well die laughing."

Joey turns to Petey and says, "Okay wise guy, let me see if you can catch an eel." He picks up a squirming live eel out of the tank and throws it at him.

"C'mon Joey, that's enough! Frankie is coming any minute. He said he'd be in at noon to check on us. He'll kill us! Look at this mess! Joey picks up another eel and throws it at Petey. They are laughing hysterically when a long black Cadillac pulls up near the store. Frankie gets out. He is impeccably dressed in a designer Bernini suit. He hates the smell of fish, so he parks his Cadillac a half block down the street away from the store. He puts on a long plastic raincoat over his clothes so they won't get the smell of fish on them. Only his designer shoes stick out at the bottom. He walks around to the other side of the car and opens the door for his girl, Angie. She is dark-haired and beautiful. She takes Frankie's hand and they walk into the store together.

Frankie looks around at the mess, shakes his head at the two clowns and says, "What are you guys doin'!? You ruined the store! You killed the fish! If papa sees this, he'll have a heart attack. Dammit, get this place cleaned up, now!"

"Ah, we were just havin' a little fun, Frankie," says Joey. "It's not as bad as it looks."

Joey notices Frankie's raincoat. "Love your raincoat." Joey and Petey laugh. Making a face, Frankie turns up his nose at the odor, pulls a spray bottle from his pocket and starts squirting deodorizer all around Joey and Petey and the store. The spray smells like Christmas trees. "Get this place cleaned up and quick! It stinks!!"

"Yeah", says Joey, "it stinks like Christmas trees!"

Petey and Joey hustle to get the mess cleaned up. Frankie starts toward the phone to make some calls for his bookmaking business when Harvey, the linen man, enters the store.

Frankie says, "Pop ain't here, Harvey. Whadya want?"

"I've delivered towels and aprons for months and I haven't been paid! Pete told me only to go to his brother, Joe, for my bill - that he's the bookkeeper and I am to deal with him. But his dark eyes scare me. I'm afraid to tell him, but he's gotta pay!"

Frankie pulls a wad of money out of his pocket and says, "Here, will this cover it?"

146

Harvey says, "Gee, thanks buddy! Thanks a lot!" His face is lit up as he turns to leave, he's so happy that he finally got paid.

Frankie peels more money out of the wad of bills he's carrying. He turns to Joey and puts some money in his hand. "Joey, go down to Fulton Fish Market and replace the fish you ruined. Do it now! Petey, you finish cleanin' up this mess. I gotta get outta here! I'm too warm in this raincoat and I can't stand the fuckin' smell another minute!" He turns to Angie. She has been standing there, flabbergasted, with her mouth open. "C'mon, Angie, let's go. See you guys. And please, SELL the fish, don't play ball with em!" He and Angie leave the store and Frankie gestures to heaven with his hands as though praying for a miracle.

....

Early the next morning, Papa Joe is alone in the store. He's not open for business yet, but Sol the Tailor taps on the front door and Joe lets him in.

"Hi Sol, nice day, eh? I just made fresh coffee and I have apple strudel just for you."

"Hello, my friend. I need a break from that tailor shop. My eyes are tired and red and the day didn't even start yet. And prices, Joe, why are prices going up, all the time going up on everything? I remember a couple of years ago when I bought a new Chevy for $1900. Now, forget it."

As Joe serves the coffee and strudel, he says, "The world has changed Sol, now we gotta change too."

"Yeah, but it's not so easy at our age . . . Joe, not to change the subject, but when you went home early the other day, I looked in the market and couldn't believe my eyes. Your sons were throwing fish at each other and all over the store."

"Those kids will kill me yet, Sol. Mrs. Goldstein called my house and told me that she walked in and fish went flying over her head. Now, she'll only come in the store when I'm here."

"I wonder who's more miserable, Joe - me with my wife, or you with your boys? Sarah bought me a bottle of Geritol. She says I'm always tired. She says, *'Sol, let's go play bingo. Sol, let's go to Synagogue.'* I say, *'Sarah, after 35 years of marriage, you go alone'.* So, Joe, I guess we all have problems. Thanks for the coffee. I'm gonna go open the shop."

Frankie arrives and Papa Joe says, "Hey Frankie, what are ya doin' here so early? The race track not open yet?"

"Hi Papa. I'm gonna meet Petey so we can go pick up his school records."

Joey and Petey walk in the door and Joey says, "Hey Frankie, don't forget to bring the teacher an apple."

"Look, just polish your mirror Romeo so you could see yourself better. C'mon Petey, let's go get your records and say goodbye to your favorite Principal."

"Now, don't start no trouble, Frankie," says Papa Joe. "Just help Petey get straightened out, capeesh?"

Joey says, "Petey, where the hell'd you get those yellow pants? You look like a duck, a tall duck."

"See you guys. C'mon Petey."

....

When Frankie and Petey arrive at the school, there's a big commotion inside. Four teaches have gathered around and are looking down at Mrs. Sower who has fainted and is lying on the floor. They are all staring at her once beautiful mahogany desk which has been cut in half and is now lying next to her in two pierces. One of the teachers is giving her smelling salts. As she comes around, she says, "Oh, my God! Oh, my God, my beautiful desk, my heirloom!" Frankie and Petey move closer so that Mrs. Sower can see them.

"Hi Mrs. Sower," says Frankie. "What are ya doin' on the floor? Well, I hope you feel better now. Oh, and thanks for Petey's records."

Frankie and Petey smile, shaking their heads as they leave the school.

"What the hell happened?" asks Petey. "She looked like a submarine, lying on the floor all stretched out like that."

"I guess someone had their reasons," says Frankie . . .

....

Either Papa Joe or Pete goes to Fulton Fish Market early each morning to get fresh fish. When they can't go, Frankie takes his beat up truck, leaving his Cadillac parked on a side street so it won't get the fish smell inside. Outside Fulton Fish Market there's a big fire barrel that people use to keep warm and there's usually guys around it in a crap game. That's all Frankie has to see and on this particular morning, he gets in the game and comes back broke with no fish, no money, no nothing. Pulling up outside Papa Joe's, Joe comes out, saying, "C'mon open the tailgate, Frankie, and let's get the fish outta there before they go bad."

"I lost the money, Pop."

"Whadya mean you lost the money? You got no fish?! What am I gonna do with you? I give you money for the fish and you got your own money too. What are we gonna do? The people are waiting."

"Dad, what could I do? It was a loser seven, but don't worry about it, I'll go back and get the fish."

Frankie goes to his secret stash, gets more money and goes back to Fulton Fish Market. When he gets there, there's no fish. The market closes at 7:00 AM and any fish that's not sold is put out on the sidewalk. The Chinese guys come at exactly 7:00 AM and buy the fish for a nickel a pound and stuff it in their trucks. It's called "sidewalk fish" and that's what they use in the Chinese markets. Papa Joe doesn't stand for any "sidewalk fish" in his fish market.

So, Frankie goes to several fish stores in the surrounding areas and buys up all the fish he can at double and triple the prices of Fulton Fish Market and Papa Joe is happy when he returns with fish.

CHAPTER SEVEN

"CORONA PAYBACK"

At Spaghetti Park, Joe Basilio, 56 years old, is walking away from Bocce Court, waving goodbye to friends and to his brother Pete who is now 59. A green Olds pulls up and the driver spots Joe. Peppers gets out of his car and walks over to Joe. He isn't oddly handsome anymore. He's only 50 years old, but looks 60 and he's lost any charm he may ever have had.

"Hi Joe, nice day, huh? Hey, I've gotta go to Forrest Hills to pick up somethin' for my chick. Wanna take a ride? It's only half an hour or so. C'mon, keep me company."

"Only half an hour? Okay, I've got some time to kill, why not? I'll tell you about the truck me and Pete bought for the store."

"Good." Joe gets in Peppers car. "How's the Fish Store doin'? Still a struggle? You had some bad years like me. Three years behind bars in Denamora was no joke! You know, Joe, you're the only guy who talks to me. The women in the neighborhood walk across the street when they see me. Shit, I gotta make a livin', don't I?"

"Peppers, who the hell am I to judge anybody? You took a shot. It didn't work out. Me, I'm just a workin' fool, still lookin' for my luck to change."

They drive along making small talk and Peppers tells Joe that they are almost there. "I'll park the car and get my girl's stuff and be right out." Peppers gets out of the car and Joe leans back, relaxes and closes his eyes. A few minutes later, he is startled by gun shots. He hears two shots and sees a man holding his chest and falling down in the street in front of a store. Peppers jumps in the car and speeds away.

Joe says, "What the fuck is happening?! You shot that guy!! Why'd you shoot that guy?!"

"Don't say another word, Joe, or I'll shoot ya in the head! The bastard was a cop comin' home early from work. Bad timing, but I made the score. Just shut up and forget about it or I swear I'll fuckin' kill you, you understand?!"

Joe is white as a sheet. "I didn't see anything. It's not my business. Nobody is following us. I think you're safe."

"You think *I'm* safe? Joe, you're in as deep as me. You're called an 'accomplice'. Just because you got a nice wife and kids that love you, you think you're so pure? I ain't got nothin'. If I go, you go. Take some money out of the bag, Joe, we're in this together."

"I think I'm gonna throw up. I've gotta open the window," says Joe. Peppers looks at Joe and smiles a stupid crazy grin.

....

The neighborhood corner news stand is doing brisk business selling papers today. The morning headlines read:

"COP KILLED COMING HOME FROM WORK"

Behind the news stand, a radio is blasting and the newscaster is saying, "*A witness saw the first three numbers of the license plate. Police say it's just a matter of time before they catch them.*"

Joe Basilio's house is on 51st Avenue. Joe and Connie are in the kitchen and Joe tells Connie, "Call Mom and Uncle Pete and Frankie! This can't wait another minute! I don't know how to start this." He is visibly shaken.

Shortly, everyone arrives and gathers around the table. They're all speaking at once: "What's wrong? What's the matter? What is it?"

Joe gestures to them to sit down. And he begins, "Yesterday, I was at Spaghetti Park and my friend Peppers pulls up and asks me to take a ride with him to pick up some stuff - a gift for his girl, he said. I replied 'okay.' But instead of picking up a gift, he stuck up a store and came out with a gun in his hand. He shot an off-duty cop!" Joe stops and takes a deep breath. "I saw the cop fall over and die. Peppers said that if I say one word about it, he'll kill me. I was so scared. I vomited all over his car door. Anyway, I can't rat on him. I read the paper and they're ready to I.D. him - and the other person - ME!"

The family all start yelling and screaming and crying. Connie embraces Joe and buries her head in his chest, sobbing.

Frankie says, "Dammit everybody, be quiet! Let's think about this. Dad, we know who he is, so it's no secret. Peppers was always bad news, but it's too late now to worry about that. I gotta get my pal, Lou, on the phone. You remember Lou, Ma, from when I was a kid?

Good guy, Lou. He stuck with the books and he's a top lawyer now. Look Dad, even though you're innocent of this and you never even got a traffic ticket, anybody connected with a cop killer is in serious trouble. It's very dangerous for you, Pop." Frankie gets up to call the lawyer.

Connie says, "What are we gonna do, Joe? You're innocent! Go to the police station and tell them your story."

Joe shakes his head, not knowing what to do.

Frankie says, "Mom, I gotta get the lawyer to go and make arrangements with the cops for Dad to turn himself in. Dad, I don't know exactly how to help you right now, but I promise you it'll all come out all right."

Joe is shaken, but shows faith in Frankie by nodding agreement.

Gramma says, "That sonovabitch crook is ruining my son's life! I hope he burns in hell!!"

Weeping into her handkerchief, Connie starts to cry again. Joe and Pete are huddled in whispered conversation. Frankie goes to make the phone call to the lawyer.

On the phone with Lou Duro, Frankie says, "Lou, I gotta see ya right now. It's a life or death situation! Understand? Lou, I don't give a fuck who's there! Get in your car and come over to my house. Now! Yeah, I'm fuckin' excited! Lou, don't make me become a tough guy, okay? Please. Yeah now, dammit now, Lou!!"

Frankie goes back into the kitchen and sits next to his father. "Dad, go over to Uncle Pete's house and stay there 'til I come with the lawyer. Don't open the door for anyone. I don't want our family abused here. Mom, if they hit the door, don't argue with them, just say that Joe is not home, but that he will be at the police station later today.

Frankie escorts his father to the door with Uncle Pete. He watches as they drive away. Back inside the house, he is sitting quietly and sullenly with Connie and Gramma awaiting the arrival of Lou Duro.

....

The police are searching every room of Peppers house. Peppers, whose real name is John Graziadei, has disappeared. An "All-Points Bulletin" has been issued. The green Olds has been found. The cops are talking to each other as they search: *They found the Olds. It's been dusted for prints. There's another person. Two sets of prints"* . . .

....

Only a few cops are on duty at the police station later that day when the lawyer Lou Duro, Joe Basilio and Frankie arrive at the station. Before turning him in, Lou took pictures of Joe's entire body in case they start punching and kicking the "Cop Killer".

Lou steps up to the desk Sergeant. "Call the Captain and tell him to come down and we'll surrender Joe Basilio on his charges. And by the way, I took pictures. There's not a scratch on this man's body." The desk Sergeant has a puzzled expression on his face and does not appear to be aware of Joe's identity. "This better be real important. The only reason I'm calling my Captain is 'cause I recognize you, Mr. Duro. You're an important guy." "Thanks Sarge, I owe you one," says Lou.

Precinct Captain McGinty comes out and shakes hands with Lou Duro.

....

In the courtroom, Joe Basilio has been tried and convicted and is about to hear his sentence. The courtroom is packed with Joe's family and friends from the neighborhood. The anxiety and torment of this entire ordeal shows on the faces of the entire family.

Judge H. Becker is presiding. He says, "Mr. Basilio, please stand." Lou Duro stands with Joe. "You have been convicted of Second Degree Murder. I hereby sentence you to the maximum term. You are to spend the rest of your natural life in the penitentiary designated by the state of New York." Judge Becker speaks to the Bailiff: "Bailiff, take the prisoner away."

The courtroom erupts and there's nearly a riot with family and friends screaming and crying as Joe Basilio is led away in handcuffs. Joe looks back at his family, shaking his head with tears in his eyes and mouths the word, "Unbelievable!"

....

The next day, Frankie is at Lou Duro's office and the two men are discussing the trial and the cost of an appeal.

Lou says, "That sonovabitch, he railroaded us! He overruled me all the way, the coldhearted bastard! I'm sick, I'm just sick about this Frankie. You'd think he had a vendetta for the old man. I swear I don't understand it. Peppers is getting what he deserves - the chair - but this, this makes me sick. We gotta find new evidence. We gotta win on the appeal."

Frankie checks his watch and gets up to leave. "I gotta go, Lou. I gotta go work my end. You take care now." Frankie pauses, "Hey Lou, do you ever get that asthma anymore?"

"Nah, I outgrew that long ago," says Lou.

"Good. Well, I'll call you soon."

The two men embrace and Frankie leaves the office.

Lou is thinking, *'Work his end.' What does he mean by that? This guy scares me.*

....

The bus is pulling through the gates of *Sing Sing* Prison as the guard waves it in. The cons get off in chains: four white guys, four blacks, two Chinese and three Mexicans. Joe gets off and looks around, dazed like a grampa at his first visit to the zoo.

One of the guards says, "Welcome to *Sing Sing*. This ain't no country club. You will all be treated the same. If you behave here, it's not so bad. If you fuck up, you'll wish you were dead, and I'm sure some of you will be. These are the rules: first, you get your new wardrobe. Next, a shave, shower and spray job for bugs. The first thirty days it's isolation. Not even your sweet mother can visit you. You shut up and listen to your superiors. There are two men to a cell. Anyone who disobeys a rule will be introduced to solitary confinement. I promise you, you won't like it. I've seen tougher guys than you cry like a baby down there. I'm Sergeant McGary. You'll meet the rest of the guards as time goes on."

....

Five weeks pass and Joe has his first visitor. Frankie is in the visiting room which has glass partitions and phones. He's trying to remain calm, but can't hide the pain and torment he feels watching his father come in dressed in his prison uniform. His voice cracks when he tries to speak.

"Papa, I'm so glad to see you. How are you?" He notices marks on Joe's face and he loses it. Raising his voice, Frankie says, "What's wrong with your face? How did you get those black and blues? And those cuts over your eye! Jesus, what happened, Papa?!"

"I got into a little argument with two guys, but I'm all right Frankie, don't worry. They took my cigarettes and my other rations. But I'm okay, really."

Frankie slams his fists down on the table and yells, "Sonovabitch! Who did this?" The guard runs over to Frankie and warns him, "Keep it down or you're outta here!"

Frankie, fighting to control his emotions, says, "Okay, I'm sorry. It won't happen again." He turns back to Papa Joe, his face red with rage. "What are their names, Papa? What else did they do?"

"Frankie please, let's change the subject. What's new with my case?"

Frankie takes a few deep breaths and looks away for a moment. "Lou is working hard on some new angles, Papa. I'm supposed to ask you to try and remember more – anything at all."

"I'll think about it again, Frankie. I got plenty a time to think."

"I wish I could do the time for ya, Papa." There's a long pause and Frankie decides to go. "I gotta go. I'm not good company today. I'm sorry Papa, but I'll be back on a better day."

Frankie gets up to leave, puts his hands up on the glass and Papa gets up and does likewise. They touch hands through the glass and Frankie's eyes overflow with tears. "I love you, Papa!"

Frankie leaves the prison, gets into his car and breaks down.

"Sonovabitch! Look what they did to my father!! I'll fuckin' kill 'em!!!" He sits quietly for a moment, pulls out a tissue and blows his nose . . . then it comes to him. "Vito," he says out loud. "I've got Vito there!"

....

The next morning, Frankie is driving over the Williamsburg Bridge to Spring Street to visit Vito's brother, Sammy. He pulls up to the house, walks to the door and rings the bell. A boy of about 12 years old answers the door. "Hello, kid. Please tell your father that I would like to see him. My name is Frank Basilio."

The boy leaves Frankie waiting at the door. Soon Sammy appears from down a hallway. He is dark, short and stocky and is clearly startled to see Frankie waiting at the door. "Hey, Frankie, how are ya? C'mon in. Somethin' wrong with Vito? Want some coffee or somethin' to eat?"

"No, thanks, Sammy, I need you to do somethin' for me."

Sammy motions Frankie to follow him to a back room. "We can talk better here."

Frankie says, "There's two rat bastards in the joint who beat up an old man, took his cigarettes and shook him down for his rations. That old man is my father. You tell Vito to handle it. He'll know what to do. The names got back to me: 'Needles' and the other piece a shit is 'Jack Nelson'." Sam is listening intently to every word as Frankie continues, "Sammy, you tell Vito that my father must not know the outcome. You understand, Sam?"

Sammy says, "I'll deliver the message exactly like you said, Frankie."

"Thanks. If you ever need me, don't hesitate."
Frankie peels off $500.

"Buy your son some presents, maybe a new bike." He grabs Sammy's hand and puts the money in it.

"Take care of your family, Sammy." He walks out, gets in his car and drives away.

....

In the courtyard at *Sing Sing*, Vito Carulia is walking toward Joe Basilio. Joe's back is to Vito. Vito is doing ten to twenty for torturing and crippling two men over money they owed him. Vito had no remorse. Said, *"I'm only sorry I didn't kill 'em both."* Vito is 37 years old, 6 feet tall and 240 pounds. He has wiry black hair and olive eyes so intense they warn you not to stare at them. He speaks broken English. Rumor has it that he comes from Naples and is a member of *La Mano Nera.* He worked for Frankie Basilio for three years doing his trade.

Vito walks up behind Joe and says, "Hey Joe, don't turn around. I want you to know you're gonna be okay. Don't worry about nothin'."

Still with his back to Vito, Joe says, "Who are you? Why are you talkin' to me?"

"We have the same friends, capeesh Paisano?"

Joe says, "We do?" He waits for an answer, but gets none. Finally, he turns around, but the man is gone . . . into the crowd.

....

Some time has passed. It's a lousy day, cold and rainy. Guys are moving around all bundled up. Some are playing basketball to keep warm. Joe Basilio lights a cigarette and turns to see Jack Nelson, "The Rapist", walking away from his partner, "Needles", who has gone under the canvas top to keep out of the rain. Suddenly, the rain gets heavier and everyone starts running toward the canvas and some shelter. A large convict steps in front of Jack, *"Cessa pe ta."* "This is for you," says Vito as he shoves a shank through the man's jacket and into his heart. There is an audible gasp as Jack falls to the ground on his face. Vito disappears into the crowd. Nobody pays much attention until a guard blows his whistle and orders everyone back to their cells. Jack is lying on the ground. There are a few gasps of breath . . . then silence.

The guards search the cells and find nothing. The cons are locked down for 48 hours, hoping that some rat will come forward. But no one liked Jack the Rapist. Few guys ever talked to him except Needles. The two of them had a lot in common. The cons call them "White Trash". They say, *"Where they come from, they're fuckin' white trash."*

....

It's Visiting Day at *Sing Sing* and Frankie is there as usual, talking to Joe on the phones in the visitor room.

"Hi Pop. It's always great to see you! You put some weight on? You look good." He smiles at his dad, happy that he has gained some weight. "Oh, before I forget, Gramma said some special prayers for you. She said you're gonna come home soon. She and Mom, they made some anisette cookies for you. I had to give the guard some first. Wait'll you taste 'em, they're great!"

Joe says, "Oh wonderful, something from home! Mom's *anisette* cookies, they're the best! Thank them for their prayers. And tell them how much it means to me, to have the cookies. God, I miss them both so much! Frankie, how's the case coming?"

"Lou finally got us on the calendar for a new hearing in four months. New things came up. I'll tell you as soon as I know."

"Okay son, but four months, that's like four years in this place! Strange things happen here, Frankie. Some guy speaking broken English standing behind me, he says *'Don't turn around.'* He had a heavy voice. He said, *'We have the same friends, capeesh?'* Then, I turned around and no one was there. And I wasn't hearing things, Frankie!"

"Ah, it must have been some guy that likes you, Pop. Anyway, I gotta go. Don't forget your cookies at the desk."

"Don't worry about that, Frankie, I won't forget the cookies. Give my love home and tell your mother to keep writing."

They touch hands on the glass and say goodbye.

....

Frankie and Corky are driving to a crap game down Horace Harding Blvd. Corky says, "It's a good thing we could reach out, Frankie. That Vito is some piece a work. He banged a lot a guys in Italy, has balls of steel. Nobody goes near him. But he's your guy, Frankie. He remembers that you're the only one who put him in action."

Nodding his head, Frankie changes the subject. "Corky, lemme send over a coupl'a trucks to the docks in Brooklyn and pick- up some swag."

Corky says, "Wait for Wednesday. A big shipment from England is comin' in. You can fill two trucks with clothes – cashmere and wool suits - the best - Petrocelli, Bernini, all from Italy."

Frankie says, "Good, we'll make a nice score. In the meantime, I hope those pricks who owe me are at the crap game!"

They drive along listening to music on the radio. "Is that Billy Eckstein singing? Hey, isn't he a Sicilian?" asks Frankie. They both laugh and pull up to a warehouse on Queens Boulevard. The guy at the gate knows them and they go through and park.

....

At *Mickey's Joint*, Frankie is talking to Aldo at a corner booth. "Aldo, you're wasting your time at nickel and dime joints. We know each other since we was kids. I trust you. I want you to come with me. I'll put you in big action. Besides, the business is getting too big for one guy and you'll make a lot of dough. You'll be protected. Nobody can hurt you, you understand?"

"*Madone* Frankie, you're serious, huh? It's a big step for me. Jesus, I don't know."

"Listen Aldo, don't answer me now. Think it over. If you say yes, that's it. Why don't you meet me here tomorrow night, we'll eat and you can give me an answer then, okay?"

"Okay Frankie."

"With a shit load a cash in your pocket, maybe we can break that gambling habit of yours. You know don't ya, Aldo, that only suckers lose?"

They hug and Aldo leaves. Frankie goes out to his car. His Rottweiler, Tessie, has been waiting for him. Frankie walks across the street, buys a Lemon Ice and brings it back for her and she jumps in the back seat and licks it all up. "Did you like the Lemon Ice, Tessie? Good girl!" Tessie is two years old, weighs 135 pounds with a huge head and body. She's completely loyal to Frankie and is never more than three feet away from him. Her sheer size alone is a big benefit in Frankie's collection business. He speaks a few words to her; she growls and moves a foot closer to the deadbeat.

Frankie drives away in his big long Caddy.

....

The next night, Frankie walks into *Mickey's Joint* and spots Corky at the bar. "Hey Cork, I'm glad you're here. I'm meeting Aldo. Why don't you stay and eat with us?

"I'd like to, but I gotta go meet my guy in Brooklyn." Corky spots Aldo entering the restaurant. "Here comes Aldo now." Aldo comes over and warmly hugs both guys.

"Corky, you look great. I heard you got some good breaks in Brooklyn. I'm really glad for ya."

"Ya know it don't come free, ya know what I mean, Aldo?"

"Yeah Cork, I know. Let's order a drink before we eat, okay?" Aldo motions to Carmen, the bartender, and Carmen says, "I gotcha guys covered."

Corky says, "Okay, I'll have one drink then I gotta go. The guy I'm meetin' don't like to wait."

Carmen brings the drinks and Aldo says, "Ah Salute!" They all three chime in and say, "Ah Salute!"

Getting up to leave, Corky says, "I'll see ya fellas. Say hello to Papa Joe, Frankie. So long Aldo."

Corky leaves the restaurant and Frankie and Aldo go to a booth to eat. The waiter, Tommy, comes right over. "Tommy, get us started with antipasto and cioppino," says Frankie.

Aldo says, "No, No, I want veal cutlets *parmigiani*. That's all. And a glass a wine."

"You got it," says Tommy and goes to the kitchen.

"Frankie, I thought about your offer and I appreciate what you said about me. I feel you're like my brother. You have always reached out for me and I owe you an explanation. Lately, my mother cries more and more about my future. She swears I'm goin' to jail or get killed. Ya know, I get lucky some times, but if I don't leave Corona, I'm know I'm gonna break her heart, you understand?"

Frankie, listening intently to Aldo, nods his head. "My girl wants to get married. I don't wanna get fuckin' married, Frankie. And I can't stop gamblin'. I gotta leave. I'll send Mom money when I can. My brother lives in Hollywood. He works as a grip and gets small parts acting."

Frankie says, "Yeah, I saw him on some TV shows."

"He says he'll help me get a job in the studios as a grip or extra or maybe doin' stunts. He says I move like a monkey."

They both laugh and Frankie says, "Aldo, I understand. I'm disappointed, but I know how you feel. Don't get fuckin' married. You're still young. Go to your brother. Maybe someday you'll be a big star! And don't worry, I'll look in on your mom. Remember, I'm here if you need me. Do you need some scratch now? Don't hesitate!"

Aldo's all choked up. "Frankie, you're makin' me fuckin' cry."

....

The guys are throwing a farewell party for Aldo and the whole crew is there. No women allowed.

"Dammit, when I see you guys, I don't wanna leave. You've been not only pals but like my family."

The waitress brings the food and drinks to the table. "With all this food and booze," says Corky, "I feel like King Arthur! Aldo, you've been a helluva friend to all of us. Everybody, raise your glasses to our friend, Aldo. To the only guy I know who could jump off a roof and not break his neck! Good luck in Hollywood! And watch those queers out there!" Everybody laughs.

"Aldo, we're gonna miss you," says Frankie. "No matter what you end up doin', you'll always be with us. And besides, the crime rate will drop now with you gone!" There's more laughter.

"No shit Aldo, when you meet all those movie stars, tell them if they want a good haircut, I'm available," says Orlando.

"This is like a funeral. I'm gonna come back a lot ya know. I'll miss my Mom's cookin' and Mickey's Clams Oregano! C'mon, let's eat before I change my mind and stay."

Junior says, "You can't do that! You know how much this shindig cost? You gotta go!" More laughs.

Bobby chimes in, "You don't have to pay anymore dues Aldo. Hell, you always owed anyway."

Aldo frowns for a second and Bobby says, "C'mon, it's a joke buddy!" Everybody laughs together and Frankie puts his arm around Aldo and pulls him to the side to talk.

"Aldo, go live with your brother Paul. He's an excellent actor. Between being a leading man and a character actor, he works a lot. I know he has contacts that could help you. And I know you're gonna do real good out there."

"Thanks Frankie for your confidence in me." He looks at his watch.

"Gee, I gotta get goin'. My plane leaves at midnight."

"C'mon, I'll drive you to the airport."

The two men leave the restaurant with Aldo saying the last goodbyes to the guys on the way out.

....

It's meeting night at the *Corona Dukes* clubhouse. Frankie is speaking about throwing a block party to raise money for Papa Joe's legal fees.

"Look guys, I just spoke to Lou Duro, our lawyer. He says it's expensive to get a sentence changed. In other words, we need a lot a scratch."

Corky says, "Okay, let's have a block party and sell raffle tickets to everybody. And I mean everybody! This weekend we get everything in order. Frankie and I will be in charge. Any major beefs, we'll handle. Bobby, you give ten books each to all our guys, ten dollars a book. That's $100 cash each. Orlando, you help Junior sell. Every store and every house gotta buy a book of raffle tickets. Bobby, you're in charge of getting the food. I'll let you know how much meat and bread and vegetables we're gonna need.

"Corky and I will get the music and PA system," says Frankie.

"Remember, everything we do is for Papa Joe's benefit. Nobody gets paid. I mean NOBODY. I wish Aldo was here to help us. He's got a way of robbing you and making you like it!" They all laugh. "Okay, anybody got any questions?"

Orlando asks, "What if some jerk won't buy a book?"

"You write the names down of any assholes that say no and they'll buy two books, I promise you," says Corky.

Bobby says, "You guys gave me a big job to do. All that food costs a lot a money. But in the end I guess it's cheaper than all their stores burnin' down, eh?" He laughs. Corky continues, "We're gonna close off 51st Avenue. I wanna get all the cars off the street and rope the street off. Anybody objects, burn their cars. They'll get the message. Frankie, talk to the ladies. Tell them, please do all the cooking for the party. I'm sure they will be happy to help."

"Okay," says Frankie, "and by the next meeting we'll have all the answers to any more questions. Meetin' adjourned. Thanks guys!"

....

The night of the block party, everything is set and in order. There are tables for sausages and meatballs, lasagna, pizza ovens, soda, beer, wine. The band is set-up and ready to make music. The street is blocked off from one end to the other. People are coming in by the droves. Frankie and his crew have set-up a temporary office at Corky's mother's house. Her name is Mary.

They're all there when someone knocks at the door. Orlando answers it.

"Hi, what can I do for ya?"

A man with a nondescript face, red hair, tall and skinny but with a strong voice and dressed in a black suit is standing there. "I'm Inspector Simmons from the Licensing & Permit Division for the city of New York."

"Hey, no kiddin'," says Orlando. "I thought you were a cop with that badge. Wait a minute, will ya?"

Orlando goes to tell Frankie and Corky about this man. Frankie and Corky go to the door. Corky says, "Hi Inspector, c'mon into the office. What can we do for ya?"

"I came to see your permit to operate this block party and close off a city street. You better have one because it's illegal what you're doing without a special permit."

Getting up close to him Frankie says, "Do you know me or my partner?"

The Inspector answers, "No, am I supposed to know you? I just want to see your permit or you'll have to vacate the block immediately."

Corky says, "Frankie, stop wasting this nice Irish man's time. Show him the permit!"

"You're right," says Frankie as he opens the desk drawer and takes out an 8 inch stiletto and puts it on the table. He reaches into his pocket, pulls out a 38 caliber revolver and puts it on the table next to the stiletto. "Inspector, this is our permit."

The Inspector's face turns white and he starts stuttering, not knowing what to say. He is visibly shaken.

Corky says, "Okay, do you want us to use our permit or why don't you just get the fuck outta here? But before you go, remember that this is the end of this meetin'. I don't wanna hear from you again or from your bosses, capeesh?"

Speaking to Frankie, Corky says, "Frankie, get some beer for this Irish guy before he passes out!"

"No, no, I'm leaving now," says the Inspector. He turns and rushes out, and Frankie, Corky and Orlando walk over to the block party. The party is coming to an end and everyone is packing and cleaning up. The kids on the street are all helping out.

Orlando says, "When you kids finish up, meet me on the corner and I'll take you all for hot dogs and pizza plus some cash for your pocket. You all did a great job!"

Bobby says, "You know Orlando you really should run for Mayor of New York. How many of those kids are yours anyway?" They both laugh.

The band leader is waiting for Frankie or Corky so he can get paid.So is the street decorator who put up the streamers and balloons. Also two Cops who kept order on the street. Corky and Frankie are walking toward the vendors. Corky says, "Are you gonna show 'em the permit? Frankie, you talk to these people. They may start cryin' or some fuckin' thing. I'm tired as a bastard. I'll go collect the money from the party."

Frankie walks over to the band leader, street vendors and the cops. He makes a speech: "I want to say to you all, you did a great job today for a special benefit. And I will never forget you, my friends. If you ever need advice or help, feel free to see me or Corky. Everyone here donated their talent and time and we really do appreciate it! Thank you very much for all your help."

Frankie turns to leave. The band leader hollers, "Just a minute! I wanna get paid! We don't work for free! And I don't know who you are and I don't care who you are!"

Frankie says, "You don't care? Okay, I'll get Junior to pay you off. Maybe he'll even give you a bonus. He'll introduce himself to you. Give me your house number and he'll come personally to pay you, okay? Anybody else wanna get paid, Junior will come see you too. He'll be happy to take care of you."

Frankie turns and leaves the disgruntled men with their faces and mouths aghast, not believing what they just heard. He walks away in perfect confidence and goes into the office to count the money they made at the block party. He picks up the phone and calls Lou Duro.

"Hey Lou, I wanna know how much the paperwork and the expense of this appeal is gonna cost. How much?" There's a long pause while Frankie raises his eyebrows and paces the floor. "Okay Lou, I'll give you that, but I'll expect your phone call tomorrow afternoon." He hangs up the phone.

....

Uncle Pete is behind the counter of Papa Joe's Fish Market cleaning fish. Sol the Tailor from next door, is visiting.

"I miss Joe, he was my friend. It's a shame what happened, such a shame! A good man like him! I really miss him."

"My brother is too nice, that's his trouble," says Uncle Pete as he's chopping the head off a fish with a big cleaver. "I'm gonna see Joe next week Sol, maybe you would like to come? I could arrange it."

"Who would watch the store for you?" asks Sol.

"Joey and Petey will watch the store."

"You trust those crazy kids, you're as crazy as them!" Sol sees a customer going into his shop next door and turns to go. Before he leaves, he says, "Okay Pete, you arrange it. I would really like to see Joe. I miss him! I really miss him!

....

It's Visiting Day at *Sing Sing* and Frankie is on the house phone talking to Joe. "Papa, you're looking so much better! Now listen, I want you to forget that incident with that man.

I don't want you involved. I don't want you to look for him. Just go about your life without worry, okay? He might be an 'Angel on your shoulder', who knows?"

"Yeah okay Frankie. So tell me, how's your mother and Gramma? Your brothers? Your Uncle Pete? God, I hope he's selling fish!"

"Everybody's okay, Dad, they just miss you so bad. The store is okay. Uncle Pete is making it work, God bless him. Mom and Gramma are always at Church praying for you to come home. Uncle Pete says to tell you he'll be visiting soon. He wants to bring good news, Pop."

"I'd really like that, it's been too long." Joe stops to think. "Look son, I know you're trying hard to get me home, but don't get into any trouble because of me. I'm doin' okay here. The food could be better. But I bunk with a nice old Chinese guy. His name is Cornel Yang. He's got four more years to do. He shot his son-in-law in a fit of rage over six Laundromats that he owned. Cornel says the sonovabitch robbed him and beat up his daughter. No wonder he had rage! Guess everybody's got a story, huh?"

The bell rings and visiting time is over. Frankie says, "Papa, you're a brave man. Now you remember what I said. Don't think about that person and don't look for him. He will find you, capeesh? When it's time, he will find you. I gotta go. Bye Dad."

They touch hands through the glass like they always do.

....

Aldo is at his brother Paul's' house in a middle class Hollywood neighborhood. They are sitting outside on the patio at a redwood table. The kids are playing in the yard.

"Well Aldo I'm glad you're here with us. Rosie has your room set-up at the back of the house away from the kids so you'll have a little more peace and quiet. Of course, you're their Uncle and they love you."

"Thanks, Paul. It's nice to have kids around, keeps your head on straight."

"Tuesday, I'm working at Paramount and I want you to see the studio and how this make-believe business works. Besides, I can introduce you to some people who might help you get started. First thing, we'll

185

get you signed-up as an extra. It won't be much, but at least you'll make some money and you'll observe how the business works."

"That would be great, Paul."

Rosie comes out and tells the guys to come on in, the ziti is getting cold and the little ones want to play with Uncle Aldo.

....

Three months pass. Aldo is learning to do stunts and is getting very good at it. He has a natural physical ability and a fearless heart, thanks to his *Corona Dukes* background. He is now being paid for taking those big chances.

At *Desilu Studio*, Aldo is doing his first pro stunt. He has to drive between two trucks at 70 miles an hour and crash into the car in front of him. He does it perfectly without any extra takes. The director and crew are applauding him. Nawaz Que, the director, says, "Aldo that was superb! I will consider you for stunt work on all of my pictures in the future. You blocked out that scene like a pro. Terrific! And besides, you look like Errol Flynn."

The following week, Paul and Aldo are at the commissary at *Paramount Studios* having coffee. Paul says, "We've got three weeks work on this picture. You have a small part, but you'll earn your SAG card. No more extra work and you'll be able to audition as an actor!"

"I didn't sleep all night trying to remember the few lines I have. I hope I don't screw up!" Aldo puts more sugar in his coffee.

"The lines will come. You'll see."

"You've got a good part, Paul, as the ship's doctor. They're gonna anchor the ship a quarter mile off Santa Monica Pier. One scene has me on the top deck watching the patients getting some exercise. One guy goes nuts and jumps over the rail about 50 feet high into the ocean."

Paul says, "Shit, that's gonna be really dangerous, falling over the rail like that! I'm glad you're not doing that stunt, Aldo!"

"I could do it, Paul. In *Corona* down by the World's Fair, you know the *Aquacade*, we used to dive off the 40 foot board, me and Orlando, all the time."

"Are you nuts? This is over 50 feet and into the ocean! It ain't no swimming pool!" Shaking his head, he says, "You scare me, Aldo, you've got no fear."

"I'm telling you, Paul, I could do it! C'mon, let's get outta here. I need to study my lines."

The next day at the Santa Monica Pier, actors and extras are boarding a launch to go out to where the ship is anchored. With them is Hollywood's top Stuntman, Don Allen, who has two more shots before the big scene. In one, there's a fight scene with the star and a patient who is a bitter G.I. The fight takes place at the top of the iron stairs of the ship. The star is to fall down the stairs and Don steps in for the stunt. Somehow he is pushed down the stairs, breaks his ankle and is "out of action". Shooting has come to a halt. The cast is standing around watching and waiting for the medics to come and take Don Allen to sick bay.

Nawaz Que, the director, is talking to the producer of the film. "Son of a bitch, I'm sorry Don got hurt, but now we're really behind schedule. We're screwed. I have nobody to do this next stunt. It's dangerous as hell.

Nobody would want to do it. It'll take some time to find the guy crazy enough to do it. I have no ideas right now."

The producer has a scowl on his face and says, "Well, you better hurry up and get some!"

Aldo overhears the conversation and says, "Nawaz, I can do it. I'll make the jump, right into the ocean. Believe me, I can do it."

Admiring the young man's spunk, Nawaz smiles, saying, "Thanks Aldo, but I need a guy with that kind of experience. And I can't be responsible for what could happen. The production could be sued and I'd be out of a job if anything went wrong. Besides, I like you."

"Then give me a shot," says Aldo. "I can do it. I'll sign a waiver releasing production of all responsibility if anything goes wrong. Please, let me do it. I won't let you down, I swear. I know what I'm doing."

"Son of a bitch, you're so positive, I believe you! I believe you can do it, but we better be right, pal. No second chances on this one."

Paul steps in, worried for his brother. "Aldo, do you know what you're doin'!? You can get killed doin' this. Fuck the stunt. Let 'em get somebody with experience."

"I know what I'm doin', Paul."

Nawaz adds, "Aldo, you do this right, you'll get all the work you can handle from here on out, believe me!"

"Let me block the scene and I'll be ready whenever you are," says Aldo.

"First thing in the morning," says the director.

Paul stands there flabbergasted and the crew breaks up to go home.

....

The next morning on the set, Aldo has the scene blocked off. Everyone is tense. Director Nawaz is a nervous wreck, chain smoking and pacing back and forth. Aldo stands waiting, eating an ice cream cone, cool as ice. The "troops" are all in position on the hospital ship. The top deck of the ship is higher than 50 feet and Aldo knows it. He's marked his spot and is ready. They start to shoot the scene . . .

Paul, as the doctor, is addressing a squad of men, telling them how to react and adjust to civilian life: *"It's a slow process, taking it easy, one step at a time."*

Suddenly from the ranks, a G.I. breaks toward the rail of the ship screaming, *"Mama, Mama"* and runs to the edge. The director cuts to Aldo's back doubling as the G.I. Aldo sails over the ships' rail and into the ocean, smooth as silk. Down below, frogmen and cameramen in boats are ready for any emergency. The director yells, "Cut, cut!!!! Is he coming up?!!!!!" Nawaz looks over the rail down into the water with all the other crew members. Aldo is bobbing up out of the swelling ocean, surrounded by the frogmen, a small boat and the cheers and applause of all around and above him, like it was the end of the Super Bowl! Nawaz' face shows relief and gratitude. "Aldo, Aldo, great job! Perfect! Thank you! Thank you! You did it, you crazy bastard! You did it!!

....

At Spaghetti Park in *Corona*, Frankie and Corky are eating a watermelon. Corky asks, "Did you hear from Aldo yet? How's he doin' out there in Hollywood?"

"Unbelievable! As a Stuntman, he's knockin' 'em out," says Frankie.

"No kiddin'? That's somethin'!"

"He wants me to come see him," says Frankie. But I can't right now. Cork, I gotta ask you a big favor. You know that prick in Denamora, Peppers? You know he's gonna get the chair. He don't give a shit about helpin' Papa get out. You know Papa, he's a piece'a bread. I wish I was in that joint for ten minutes, I'd make that Peppers squeal like a pig."

"All right, all right, relax," says Corky. "I've got three of my guys from Brooklyn in there. I'll reach out and get the bastard on his knees. He'll talk like a girl when they finish with him. I'll get the message to those guys on Tuesday, and by Wednesday you'll get an answer – Thursday at the latest."

"Corky, you're right there, since we was kids . . . let me tell you what the lawyer said about Papa's chances. They ain't good at all."

....

Its morning exercise in the *Denamora* prison yard and the inmates are feeling frisky because of the chill. Guys are running and playing basketball. Some are shadow boxing. Peppers is walking around the yard. Two guys are in the crowd. A skinny con runs into Peppers and kicks him in the balls. As he does this, he says. "Send Joe home, prick!"

Peppers doubles over and falls to the ground. As he tries to get up, another con, a big monster guy, jumps on his leg, breaking it at the shin. The skinny con punches him in the face and spits on him.

The P.A. system starts screaming: "*Everybody lay flat on the ground now!*" Guards fan out all over the place with their shotguns and whistles blowing. Order is eventually restored in the yard and the guards march the prisoners back in for lock down. Peppers is being lifted to a stretcher by the medics and two guards.

"Oh man, it hurts! Take it easy with that leg," Peppers screams in pain.

In the prison infirmary, Peppers leg has been put in a cast and dressings have been applied to his busted head. He asks, "How long am I here? Those fucks, they'll pay in blood!"

Frankie yells, "Hey Dickie, you leave that guy alone and come over here." The guy already has a bloody nose and he's relieved to have the fight broken up. He runs. Frankie yells, "You're gonna scratch my car, you little prick!"

Dickie walks over to where the guys are. "Hey Cousin Frankie, how you doin'? *Madone*, what a car! You're the first guy in *Corona* with a new Cadillac!"

"Yeah. Hey, I'm glad you're here, Dickie." Frankie asks the guys to move away from the bench so he can sit with Dickie. "Look Dickie, you've got your mother and father nuts. Your mother called me sayin' no one can control you. What am I gonna do with you? First, I gave you my customers at the junk yard. Then you took 'Joey N's' customers, plus you beat up two of his guys. They don't belong to you! You were told to leave those people alone. You sent the message back, sayin' *'Fuck You,' 'I don't take orders from you!'* Dickie, do you know that Corky had to step in and tell them you're my cousin? He also apologized for you. You were gonna be 'history' at the end of the week! Did you know that? These are 'made guys', Dickie!"

Frankie lights a cigarette and continues. "Now that I've got ya here, what's this shit about you wanna kill some guy because you love his wife? Are you really fuckin' crazy? You're just a kid, and you got no business talkin' like that, do ya hear me?"

"I know you're mad Frankie, and you're right, but first lemme tell you what happened: At the junk yard, some guy jumped out of a car with a bat. What was I supposed to do, get my head broke? So I gave him and his friend a beatin'. I don't know who they are Frankie. The other thing, this girl, I really love her and her two kids! The husband is a construction worker. He comes home and beats her and the kids everyday like clockwork. It's true she's older than me, but Frankie I think about her all day long. I can't get her outta my mind! So that's why I gotta kill the prick."

"Enough of this, you listen to me Dickie. First, ya gotta apologize to those guys and I gotta be there. You owe one guy $500 for breakin' his teeth. He needs a dentist bad. And second, you don't fuck with their customers, understand? If you have any problems, don't use your hands. You call me and I'll handle it, okay? And Dickie, isn't there somethin' else you wanna do with your life? I mean it. I'll help you out."

"Cuz, you're gonna laugh at me, but you know what I'd like to do? I'd like to be an actor. That's crazy, isn't it?"

"No, it's the first thing you said right, Dickie. Look at Aldo. He's a top stuntman in Hollywood now. Doin' fantastic! And they got some tough guys in the movies. Ya know, not all of 'em are queer? Go to acting school and try. I'll sponsor you. Just no more fuckin' up Dickie, okay?"

"You mean it, Frankie? No shit? Okay, I'll try. Who knows, maybe I'll be another Brando or Bogart!"

"Dickie, about that lady with the husband and the two kids, promise me to stay away from them for six months. Can you do that? If you tell me at the end of six months that you still love her, I'll whack the prick myself and you could marry her, okay?"

"You mean it? You really mean it, Frankie?"

"Did I ever lie to you?"

....

Gramma is going up the steps to the Convent where the Nuns live, next to St. Leo's Church. She goes every day to pray. Today, she has a basket of homemade *biscotti's*. She rings the bell and Sister Maria Conchetta answers, smiling when she sees Gramma. But Gramma doesn't smile back. She is too sad.

"Good Morning, Sister Maria. *Coma Sta?* I bringa' you some *biscotti* I make just last night."

"Oh, thank you! Bless you, Karina. Come in and sit. What's wrong? You look so sad, so depressed. Are you feeling all right, dear?"

"Oh Sister, my heart breaks about my Joe. I pray all day and night for him. He is an innocent man who took a ride with that bad man, Peppers Graziadei. Now my family is so miserable!"

"I know, I know. I am so sorry. That man, his name is Graziadei? It is familiar to me. It means, 'Thank God' in Italian. But it's more than that, there's something else . . . Karina, did he have a family, children?"

"No, he's a bastard", says Gramma. "He's got nobody."

"I'm going to ask Mother Superior anyway. She's been here almost 37 years. She would know of him or his family."

"Oh thank you Sister! It is so good to visit with you. It is so comforting. I hope you like the *biscotti's*. Now I must go to Mass."

Gramma gets up to leave and the two ladies hold hands and say their goodbyes.

Later that evening, Sister Maria telephones Gramma from her office at the Convent.

"Hello Karina, I want to thank you again for the delicious *biscotti's*. Oh, and Karina, that man Graziadei, I knew I remembered that name. Mother Superior said he did have a baby son. He brought him to our orphanage many years ago. The baby was in our care until he was two years old. He was adopted by a well-to-do family."

On the other end of the phone, Gramma says, "Oh, I didn't know."

Sister Maria continues, "Yes, the couple adopted the baby and moved away. That's more than I should tell you, Karina, but you see, I haven't lost my memory yet, dear friend!" She pauses and chuckles. "Well dear lady, I must go. I am praying for you and your family. Goodnight now."

With a shocked and somewhat puzzled expression on her face, Gramma says, "Goodnight Sister."

....

The next morning after Sister Maria's phone call, the family is having breakfast. Frankie says, "Mom, you make the best sausage and eggs in the world!"

Gramma tells everyone, "I brought the Sisters some *biscotti's* yesterday at the Church. Guess what? Sister Maria remembers the name, that bastard Peppers name, Graziadei. She knew it meant 'Thank God' in Italian. Mother Superior thinks he had a son, a baby in their orphanage years ago."

Frankie almost chokes on his eggs. "Are you sure, Gramma? It's the same guy, Peppers? This could be very important for us."

"The Sister said some rich couple adopted the baby boy when he was two years old. It was more than she should tell me, so I don't know, Frankie. But that's what she said. But I don't know."

Frankie gets up and squeezes Gramma's cheeks and kisses her. "Gramma, you should be a detective! I think we may have found a way. Oh, if this is true!"

"It may be just a coincidence," says Connie. "Please don't start aggravating the Sisters, Frankie. Here, have another piece of sausage."

"No Mom, I gotta go! I got things to do," says Frankie. He hugs both women and hurries out the door.

....

That evening, Frankie visits Sister Maria at the Convent. She greets him in the Vestibule.

"Sister, I'm sorry to interrupt your evening, but I had to speak to you. I'm Frank Basilio. I'm Karina Basilio's grandson."

"Yes, of course," says Sister Maria. "We are so sorry about your Father and pray that he will be coming home soon. How can I help you?"

"Sister, you said to Gramma that Peppers Graziadei had a baby son that was adopted by some very nice people. I need to speak to them about the baby they adopted. I am desperate, Sister. My father isn't well. He is dying in that prison because of Peppers. He looks ten, fifteen years older and the young prisoners take advantage of his age. They take his cigarettes and rations and even his food from his plate. This might be the only chance he gets! Please, Sister!"

202

"Mother of God, I am so sorry, Frank! But what can I do? We in the Church cannot give out anyone's name. Not that kind of information. I don't know what to say, my son. I can't break my vows and I can't see a poor soul suffer for nothing he has done. Please, let me pray about this. I will pray for God to guide me." She hesitates a few moments in deep thought then she says to Frankie, "Call me tomorrow after 4 o'clock. I will be finished with my prayers and I will give you an answer. A very difficult answer it will be. But God will help me now. I am in a grave situation." Sister Maria reaches out to shake Frankie's hand.

"God Bless you, Sister Maria. I have faith. God is fair. *He* will tell you what to do. Goodnight now."

....

The next day inside the Convent, the Sisters are finishing up from prayers. Sister Maria goes to the privacy of her office. No sooner does she sit down at her desk than the phone rings. It is Frankie Basilio calling.

"Hello Frank. Yes, yes. Can you come down to the Rectory? There will be a Prayer Book on the desk with your name on it. Take it and turn to page 37. I don't know if tears of joy or tears of sorrow await me, but I am praying for you and your family. Goodbye Frank."

Frankie hangs up the phone, rushes out of the house to his car and drives the few blocks to the Church. He is out of the car almost before it's in park and runs into the building, out of breath. There is a package at the front desk for him. He sees his name on it, "*Mr. Frank Basilio*". No one is there to see him. He takes the package, feeling like a thief in the night, quickly turns and walks to his car. When he is safely in his car, he locks the doors and opens the Prayer Book to page 37. He reads the note aloud to himself:

> *Dear Frank,*
>
> *I have prayed through the night and God said to me, "the outcome will be my reward". I want to see my dear friend, Karina, smile again.*
>
> *The name and address are:*
>
> *Mr. & Mrs. Jack Ecker*
>
> *811 Bell Avenue*
>
> *Plattsburg, N.Y.*

Frankie clutches the note to his chest and says to himself, "Maybe your luck will change now, Papa."

....

Joe Basilio is sitting alone on a bench in the prison yard. He doesn't look good. He sneezes and blows his nose repeatedly. His eyes are closed like he's a million miles away. His Chinese cell mate, Cornel, comes over to the bench where Joe is sitting.

"Hey Joe, what are you doing alone out here? Don't you feel good? Maybe you should see the doctor or something?"

"No, Cornel, I'm just real unhappy. My kid and our lawyer, they're workin' like hell to help me. But it's a bitch, Cornel. Looks like I'll die here, huh? Maybe sooner than I think."

"Don't give up, Joe. You'll get a break. Boy, that fuckin' Judge, he really screwed you!" Cornel glances off to the side where he sees a man approaching them. He recognizes Needles. "Hey Joe, that rotten Needles is comin' over. It's shakedown time. He's a born troublemaker. They tried to kill that lowlife creep twice, but the guards were on it too quick. It's tough to do in here, but I wish I could."

Needles walks over to the bench where Joe and Cornel are sitting. "Hey old man, it's cigarette time. And leave the fruit on your plate tonight, that's for me too. How come you hang out with this Chink? You're a Wop, aint you? And you, Chink, you're a foreigner. You don't even belong in this Country. I was born white – an American from Arkansas - so fuck you Chink!"

As Needles walks away, Cornel says to Joe, "See what I mean? How could you feel good with trash like that bothering you? Joe, I learned in my life that 'what goes around comes around'. Someday, he'll mess with the wrong guy and the world will sleep a little easier. Rumor has it he's gonna be transferred. He's a marked man. Hey, aren't you hungry? It's time for lunch. Let's go, friend." The two men walk off together.

....

Frankie is in his black Cadillac pulling into the city of Plattsburg in upstate New York. He stops by the side of the road to study his map for a few minutes then pulls away. *811 Bell Avenue* is the address of a large English Tudor house in an upscale neighborhood. Frankie parks out front and walks up to the front door where he rings the bell. An elegant, soft-spoken lady with silver gray hair answers the door.

"Excuse me Ma'am, but are you Mrs. Ecker?"

"Why no, I'm not. The Eckers moved away years ago. I don't have any idea where they moved to. Are you a relative?"

"A long lost cousin. I sure would love to see them."

"Well, I know they have a son who is a prominent attorney in town. His name is Jack Jr. He's running for some big political office, Mayor or something. I'm sorry I can't be of more help . . ."

"Thanks Ma'am, you've been a big help. I'll check out Jack Jr. Goodbye now."

Frankie turns and literally runs to his car. His sits for a moment, thinking then starts the car and drives off. He drives to the business section of town and finds a phone booth with a local public telephone book inside. He looks in the Yellow Pages under "Attorneys" and finds "Jack Ecker, Jr." listed. He finds the nearest gas station. Inside, he talks to the Proprietor.

"Say, do you know how to get to 863 South Main Street from here?"

"Sure, that's right straight downtown, *The Lawyers Building*. Just hang a right at the light, go two blocks, make a left and that's Main Street then go about two miles and you're there. You can't miss it."

Frankie pulls away toward Main Street and finds *863 South Main*. It's a big stone building surrounded by trees and flowers with steps going up to the entrance. Frankie drives around the block several times before finding a parking space. He puts some coins into the parking meter and enters the building, scanning the directory for the name of Jack Ecker, Jr. He finds him listed on the 10th Floor, Suite 1020.

There are several people on the elevator. Frankie doesn't seem to be aware of anyone or anything. He is visibly irritated as the elevator makes several stops to let people on and off before finally arriving at the 10th Floor. He gets off the elevator and enters the Offices of Jack Ecker, Jr. A beautiful red-haired receptionist greets him. She could be in the movies.

"Hi, I'm sorry but I have no appointment. I'd like to see Mr. Ecker. I came in from out of town. It's a personal matter and it's very important."

"May I have your name, please?"

"Frank Basilio"

"Just a minute, sir."

She goes into Jack Ecker's private office and comes back within moments. She has a surprised look on her face. "He said he would see you. Mr. Ecker will see you in a few minutes, sir. Please have a seat and make yourself comfortable."

Frankie scans a few pages of a magazine and glances back at the receptionist a few times before Jack Ecker comes out to see him. He is average height, a few pounds overweight. He has brown hair and blue eyes with a high forehead just like Peppers. He even has Peppers large nose.

"Come in, Mr. Basilio. I have a few minutes to see you."

The two men enter Jack Ecker's private office. It's plush with a mahogany desk and leather chairs. A wet bar is at the right side of the room.

"Have a seat, Mr. Basilio. Would you like a drink, some coffee?"

"No thanks, Mr. Ecker. I came from *Corona* in Queens. As you know, my name is Frank Basilio. I've got a strange story to tell you. Maybe you should have that drink? I don't know if you've heard my name or have heard of me?"

"The name rings a bell. Are you the same man who's been in the newspapers quite often? Involved with organized crime? Your father is in *Sing Sing* for Second Degree Murder? His partner is getting the chair?"

"Yeah, you do your homework. You lawyers have a great pipeline of information. That saves us a lot of time. I'm here to ask for your help."

"My help? Why would I want to help you? You're not my client, not even a friend or acquaintance. Why?"

"I don't know how to talk in circles, Mr. Ecker, so let me tell you why I'm here. Many years ago your father put you in an orphanage. You were adopted when you were two years old by Jack and Alice Ecker. They raised you and put you through Law school. Now you are an important man and I'm sure a good and kind person."

Jack is very agitated now, on the verge of losing his temper. "Just hold on! Who the hell are you to walk in here and disrupt my life and know so much personal information about me? Are you looking for trouble? I mean, do you know what I do?!"

Frankie, keeping his cool says, "Jack, I know what you do. Do you know what I do? If you know that, do you think this office and your great leather chairs and that pretty broad outside can protect you? Do you? I would suggest you calm down and let me finish. I have another really big surprise for you."

Realizing the danger he could be in, Jack changes his tone of voice and his attitude. "Please go on, tell me the rest. I'm sorry I lost my temper."

"The man who is guilty of murder and is going to die in the electric chair, the man who convinced a judge that Joe Basilio was as guilty as him, that man is your father. Do you understand that, Jack?"

Jack turns white and starts shaking like a leaf. He grabs his chair and sits down to keep from falling. Frankie keeps talking. "My father didn't do a damn thing except take a ride with that prick. He said, '*Joe Basilio was my partner'* in the stick-up robbery. My father never did an illegal thing in his life. He worked like a bastard to feed a family that he loves. Now he's doin' life in *Sing Sing* because of your father!"

"I feel dizzy. I need a drink. Please Mr. Basilio, open that cabinet over there and get the Scotch whiskey and two glasses." Jack takes out a handkerchief and wipes beads of perspiration off his face. Frankie pours the Scotch and hands a glass to Jack and takes one for himself. Jack gulps his down and continues talking. "I'm completely overwhelmed. I can't believe this is happening to me!"

"Are you okay? You're as white as a ghost. Anyway, Jack, I'm asking you for a favor. I need you to go see your father in *Denamora* and do what lawyers do. Explain to him who you are and maybe he'll change his mind and attitude when he knows you're his real and only son. Right now, he has no idea who you are. You might shock him into reality when he sees you." Frankie pauses to sip on the Scotch. "It would be to your advantage, Jack, if you were to get this done for me. Tell him to go to the warden and do the first good thing in his life. TELL THE TRUTH ABOUT JOE BASILIO!"

"What if I don't? You're expecting me to expose my whole life for a man I never knew. What if I don't?"

"You might say Jack, as a last resort, and if your pleading is not enough, that he will have blood on his hands for the death of his son he never knew. Italians believe in 'an eye for an eye' Jack."

"Anyone else, I'd call the police and have you arrested. But I know better. I'll do what I have to do."

At the exclusive Bayside Country Club, a large sign over the front door reads:

"Lawyers and Judges Ball AKA Legal Beagles"

Inside, the tables are set with exquisite white Irish Linen, candles, fine china and crystal. Soft music is playing and the atmosphere is one of privilege and entitlement. "Reserved" signs are on each table with name cards for the guests. Lou Duro is seated with his wife Doris, and two other couples, Mr. and Mrs. Bob Mason and Mr. and Mrs. John Moffitt. Lou's table is surrounded by other tables, but there is plenty of room for guests to visit and chat with other guests. At Lou's table, they are toasting each other.

Lou is talking about who got fat and who lost weight.

"I've tried to quit eating so much Italian food but I find it impossible to go more than a couple of days without some pasta and meatballs. Why is it that all good food is fattening as hell? I just buy bigger clothes." He laughs at himself.

Bob Mason says, "Lou, you and in fact all of us should be happy that we're here and in reasonably good

213

health. There's poor Vincent Lamb at the next table. He's just recovered from open heart surgery and he's only 45 years old! That's young. He took his job home each night and the stress got to him."

"Yeah, and he was on the verge of a divorce," says Lou. "That got to him too."

Bob nods his head about the divorce and then takes a few sips of his drink and continues talking. "The worst incident I know among lawyers and judges is my friend Herbert Bloomberg. His career almost ended before it began. He had a head-on collision that very nearly killed him."

Everyone is listening intently as Bob tells about his friend, Herbert Bloomberg. Lou is sipping his martini and stirring the olive.

"It was just before he became a judge. The guy was laid up almost a year. Had all kinds of reconstructive surgery. They had to fix his whole face. I mean new nose, new cheeks. He looks like a different man. He lost 40 pounds and he's kept it off." Gesturing to his right, Bob says, "There he is three tables over to the right. He even changed his name after the accident. Herbert Bloomberg became H. Becker. You've heard of H. Becker, the Judge? He's lucky to be alive!"

Lou Duro has choked on his olive and is coughing up a storm. He's shocked, but tries to cover it up. Still coughing, he says, "Excuse me please, I swallowed the wrong way. Yeah, my God, I know H. Becker. I was in front of him on a case. He had no mercy and no compassion for my client."

John Moffitt adds, "You know Bob, now that you mention it, I do remember him. He was a fat guy and had a large pushed-in nose, like a fighter's nose."

"He looks better now, huh?" Bob asks. Sensing that the women are being left out of the conversation, Bob tries to now include them. "Gee gals, I'm sorry I got carried away with all this morbid stuff."

Doris turns to Lou and says, "I want to dance, Lou. Don't you girls want to dance?"

Cathy says she's getting hungry and would like some more champagne. She turns to Gloria and says, "You haven't said a word tonight, Gloria."

Gloria replies, "Well, I'm married to a lawyer!"

Everybody laughs at the remark. Lou takes Doris' hand and leads her to the dance floor. On the way out he whispers to her, "Honey, I gotta make one quick phone call. Come with me."

"Oh Lou, you promised no business tonight!"

Lou goes to the public phone, dragging Doris behind him. It's a quick call. "Hello Frankie, this is Lou. I gotta see you first thing in the morning! Okay, I'll be there. Bye."

....

Early the next morning, Lou arrives at Frankie's house. The two men are sitting in the kitchen having coffee. Frankie says, "Needles has been transferred to Folsom, Lou. He's not my priority now. So what's the urgent matter you wanna discuss? Tell me, Lou."

"Frankie, I'm gonna tell you a story that's gonna knock you out. Last night, I went to this Lawyers and Judges Annual Ball. I sat with some people, including my friend Bob Mason and his wife. He unraveled a mystery for us. He was talking about people who had unfortunate things happen to them. He told us about a lawyer who had a head-on collision in which the guy almost died. He was disfigured. Plastic surgery saved him from looking like a monster."

"So, what's the mystery, Lou? Here, have a donut, more coffee?" Lou shakes his head, "No."

"Okay, so what's the mystery?"

"The guy who was disfigured in that crash was a lawyer. He later became a judge. His name was Herbert Bloomberg. HERBERT BLOOMBERG! Do you hear me, Frankie? He changed his name to H. Becker. Herbert Bloomberg became H. Becker. New face. New name. He also lost 40 pounds. No wonder you didn't recognize the bastard!"

Frankie is reacting with a lot of emotion, pounding the table with both fists, very nearly screaming. "Sonovabitch! Sonovabitch!! All the beatings I gave him when we were kids, no wonder he hurt Papa's trial! That rat! He got even!!" Frankie keeps saying, "Sonovabitch! Sonovabitch!"

"That's why he shut me down through the whole trial, Frankie. But this could be a blessing in disguise. He should have disqualified himself. He knew you from the past. He took a shot, hoping no one would ever know. That was his payback. The New York Bar Association will be interested in this."

Frankie says, "I'll kill the bastard! Dirty rotten creep! He'll see what a payback is. His father still lives in our old house. Lou, get this handled legally now. I'll take care of the rest."

"You're not gonna go and do some dumb thing now, are ya Frankie? I know you're hot as hell, but let's move cautiously 'til we get this handled, okay pal?"

Frankie just looks at him, his eyes cold as steel.

....

In the warden's office at *Denamora Prison*, the warden is listening to Jack Ecker Jr. explain why he needs this special interview.

"I am co-counsel with Lou Duro on this case now. I have found major discrepancies that will prove that Joe Basilio was completely innocent."

"Permission is granted. I'll have the guard bring Peppers up to the visitors' room. I'll be just a few minutes," says the warden. He picks up the phone to arrange for the inmate to be brought out. Jack shakes his hand, thanking him.

Jack goes to the visitors' room and is waiting for Peppers to be brought out. He is nervous and sweating badly. Peppers enters and the two men sit at a booth and pick-up the phones.

"Who the fuck are you? Warden told me to meet you. Whadya want?" asks Peppers.

"I don't have much time, so I'll start by saying my name. It is Jack Ecker, Jr. I am an attorney. I am here to ask you to reconsider the fact that Joe Basilio is an innocent man. Speak to the warden and tell him you made a bad mistake at the trial."

"Are you fuckin' crazy? Get the hell outta here, you bum! Basilio can go fuck himself with his whole family. Me, I got nobody. Why should I care about him? At least when he dies, he's got people, a wife and kids crying on his grave. Me, I got nobody." He moves to leave.

"You're mistaken Peppers, that's why I'm here. You better sit down for this because you've got a big shock coming."

Peppers is very annoyed, but decides to hear him out.

"After I was born, you took me to St. Leo's Church and put me in the orphanage. I stayed there until I was two years old. I was adopted by Jack and Doris Ecker. They moved me to upstate New York where they raised me and sent me to college and Law school."

Peppers is highly agitated now, but he doesn't yell because of the guards. "What the hell are you talkin' about? Who told you all this shit? Where did you come from? You're sayin' I'm your father? Is this some lawyer's scam? You got no proof. Get the fuck outta here! You're not my son! This is some kind of a trap!"

"I assure you, I am your real son and it's not a trap. Take a good look at me. Look at my face." Peppers is looking at Jack intensely. "I don't like this any better than you do. My life is turned upside down. But if I don't convince you, I will be assassinated and you will have another murder on your conscience, only this time it'll be your son's."

Visibly shaken, Peppers says, "I can't listen to this shit no more! Tricksters! Bunch of tricksters! Guards, get me outta here! I can't listen no more."

The guards come to remove Peppers. On his way out, he turns to Jack and says, "My son! What a crock a shit! My son, huh?!" And he laughs as he's going out the door.

....

Frankie and Corky are walking down 108th Street toward Spaghetti Park. Frankie says, "Papa's in the hospital. He had a heart attack because of that Jew prick judge. Anyway Corky, I'm bringin' Aldo back from Hollywood. He's the best second-story man I know. Only I don't wanna rob this bastard. I need Aldo to plant some shit in his house and then get out. I trust him and he knows what he's doin'. You know, I'm gonna do the best thing in my life! I swear, I'm gonna whack this fuckin' judge!" Frankie lights a cigarette and Corky lights one too. Frankie talks with point-blank determination as they walk toward the park.

"Corky, I'm gonna come to the *Cozy Nook* and have dinner with you and Orlando and Junior on Saturday night at about 12 midnight. This is my plan, Cork." He whispers his plan to Corky and Corky says, "Don't worry, Frankie. I hope Papa makes it okay."

Still with his mind on this one thing, Frankie says, "Orlando and Junior might guess, but they don't know. We'll leave it that way, Cork. I owe you brother!"

"Ah Fongool! What are we, strangers Frankie? C'mon, I'll buy you a Lemon Ice 'cause I'm a big sport."

They walk toward the Lemon Ice Stand laughing.

....

Early the next morning at Frankie's house, he's talking on the phone with Aldo in Hollywood.

"Yeah, Aldo, a lot a things are different now. It's been a year, can you believe it? I heard you're doin' stunt work and small parts. I'm really proud of ya, buddy! I bet ya got plenty'a broads to do some stunts with, eh?" Frankie laughs and listens to Aldo on the other end of the phone.

"Yeah well, Aldo, remember what we spoke about before you left? You said if I ever need you, you'd drop everything and come back. Well, I need you now for an important thing. I'll tell you when you get back to Corona. Aldo, it means a great deal to me." Frankie pauses again, listening to Aldo.

"I'll never forget this, Aldo. Call me and no one else and I'll pick you up at the airport. Thanks pal!" Frankie hangs up the receiver.

....

Frankie and Aldo are driving to *Corona* from the airport in the black Cadillac. Aldo says, "It must be serious boss to need me back. Anyway, I'm glad to see you, buddy!"

Frankie says, "Aldo for your own good I'm gonna tell you only what you need to know, okay? Don't ask questions. I'll tell you the plan." Aldo nods his head, "okay" and Frankie talks methodically now. "I want you to get into a certain house. 'Slim Jim' the front door or try the patio doors. You'll have plenty of time. I don't want it to look like a robbery or a break-in. When you're in, you plant two bags of coke. Break one and spread it around in the drawer in the bedroom. I'm gonna give you $2,000 in phony money: four $500 stacks. Rub coke on 'em too then wipe it off. Put clothes on top of the money and close the drawer. You got it, Aldo?"

Aldo nods and Frankie says, "Are you sure?" Aldo nods again.

Frankie continues. "Then you close the door, go outside and turn on the water hose full blast and flood the yard near the front entrance to the house. I'll be waiting near the driveway for you. Your job will be done then. Mine will start when *he* pulls into the driveway. Don't forget to keep your gloves on. Walk, don't run, to the car. If you've got any questions, Aldo, tell me now."

"I got it, Frankie. I'm excited! What a surprise that guy's got comin'. I love surprises!

"Well, you're really gonna love this one!" says Frankie.

....

In a very wealthy area of Bayside, Frankie and Aldo approach the big beautiful house and the long driveway surrounded by a manicured lawn and lush landscaping. It's a dimly lit neighborhood, more for effect than for security. Frankie pulls up near a neighbor's driveway and parks as if he's a guest. It's eleven o'clock at night. Aldo gets out of the car and goes into the house from the rear. He is in the house, doing everything exactly as Frankie told him. Ten minutes later, Aldo comes back to the car. Water is running like a river down the driveway. He gets into the car and says to Frankie, "How did you know those people wouldn't be home? I guess it's Saturday night, huh?"

"You're right, Aldo, it is Saturday night. But I read last week that the governor invited these people and some other top officials to his mansion for dinner. Nobody refuses the governor's invitations."

"*Madone*, what a house this guy's got! Man, I'd love to rob this guy! You're such a hip guy, Frankie. I see why you're a boss. I was a little nervous, but I wasn't scared."

"Aldo, I'm sure you did everything right. That's why I got you back here. Now we need to change places. You drive when I finish my job. And no speeding."

Suddenly, headlights are seen. A car is coming down the street and it pulls into the long driveway.

Aldo says, "This prick is gonna get wet! Water is over the walkway!"

"I'm sure his wife will run like a bastard into the house. In fact, I'm bettin' on it," says Frankie.

Frankie opens the car door and pulls out a 22 Magnum. It has a silencer on it. He says to Aldo, "Start the car. I'll be right back."

Judge Becker is getting out of the car and sees the water flooding down the driveway. "What the hell is this? We're flooded. Did you leave the damn hose on? My shoes and pant legs are soaking wet!"

The Judge's wife says, "Just shut up and turn off the water! I have to pee." She runs to the front door, holding her dress up. "Ohhhh, I'm ruining my shoes and my dress!" She fumbles with the keys to the door, gets the door open and slams it shut. The judge runs to the side of the house where the faucet is. Frankie is there.

"You're all fuckin' wet, Herbie!"

Herbie turns and faces Frankie. Three shots hit him, two in the head and one to the heart. Herbie falls like a crumbled cookie to the ground. Frankie glances around, walks away down the driveway and gets into the car. Aldo's eyes are lit up and wide. "Let's go, Aldo. Did you like that surprise?"

Aldo nods. Frankie smiles and puts the gun and silencer in a bag and they drive away. Aldo says, "I didn't even hear the shots, great thing those silencers!"

"It cost me $1,000 for this baby," says Frankie. "It had better work for that kind'a money. I can't wait to get rid of this car. I hate this car! If I knew who owned it, I'd give it back to 'em." They both laugh.

"Aldo, drive me to the *Cozy Nook* and drop me off. Put your gloves and sneakers in this bag with mine. When you drop me off, park the car where we said."

"Sure thing, Frankie. I'll meet you at *Mike's Junk Yard* in the morning, at eight o'clock, like we said."

....

At the *Cozy Nook*, Corky has been setting up Frankie's alibi. It's about 10:30 PM. Corky, Junior and Orlando are sitting in the second booth nearest the front door as you enter the restaurant. Orlando goes over to the waiter. "Tommy, did a girl named Joann come in looking for me yet? She's supposed to meet me here at 10:30. She's late. If she comes in, have her come over to our table."

"Sure, Orlando, I'll send her over."

"Hey Tommy, bring us Vodka rocks, Tanqueray rocks with an olive for Frankie. Junior wants the same, and a beer for Orlando," says Corky. "Oh, and bring us a nice antipasto for four. I see you're busy, so don't rush. We got time."

Corky says to the guys, "I want you guys to listen good. It's about eleven o'clock now. If anyone comes by and asks for Frankie, he just went to the Men's Room.

He didn't feel good. We're going to eat the *Antipasto* and then we'll give Tommy the dinner order about 11:30. We'll order Linguine and Clams *aldente* for me. Order some Fried *Calamari* and *Ziti aldente* for Frankie. Orlando you like *Veal Parmigiano* and order a rack of Lamb for Junior. All of that will take another 45 minutes to an hour before its ready. And don't forget, Frankie's in the bathroom. He didn't feel good."

"*Madone*, I'm hungry," says Orlando. "We gotta wait a long time before we eat!"

"Just shut up, Orlando! At 12 midnight, Junior, you go out front of the restaurant. Frankie will meet you there. Come in rubbing your hands over your face when he arrives. Orlando and me, we'll walk over to the Men's Room and start a fight. We'll turn over a table, make a bunch of noise, throw a chair, but don't hit me! Everybody will be looking at the fight when Frankie slips in through the front door. He'll walk over and start yelling at us for fighting. Everyone will see him, and we'll kiss and make-up. Frankie will give the manager $300 for disturbing the customers. We'll sit down, eat, drink and be merry!"

"We gotta go through all that shit to eat dinner?" says Junior. "I should'a brought a sandwich with me!"

Orlando gives him a knob on the head and they both laugh.

Corky says, "Okay no more fuckin' around. Remember, this is a very important piece of work. I'm glad this joint is packed. The plan will work out great!"

"There's Joe the Landlord and his wife at that table over there. He's got a ton of money." Joe the Landlord waves to Orlando and he waves back. "I think Aldo robbed his house a coupl'a years ago."

Tommy the waiter stops at the table. "I'm sorry it's taking so long, Corky. I'm swamped and the Chef is slow as shit tonight."

"Don't worry Tommy, just bring us another round when you can."

Corky looks at his watch. It's 12 midnight. "Okay, Junior, go near the front door and wait. Don't forget to rub your face when Frankie gets to the door."

"Whatever you say Cork, it's done." Junior gets up and goes to the front door. An old Louie Prima song is playing. The place is hopping. People are enjoying dinner. Five minutes pass. A car stops out front and Frankie gets out. Junior starts rubbing his face like he has Poison Ivy. Orlando goes to the back and starts yelling. Corky throws over a table. They push each other to the floor. Junior gets into it too.

Frankie jumps in and starts yelling, "What's wrong with you guys? Stop this shit now! Are you tryin' to wreck the joint? Go back to the table and get the manager over here." Frankie walks over to the people nearby and says, "Sorry folks, it was only a friendly argument."

Ralph the Manager comes over and Frankie speaks to him. "Ralph, I'm sorry my guys got outta line. Here's $300 for your trouble."

"That's okay Mr. B, don't worry about it. It's nothin' serious."

"No, I want you to have this. Buy your wife some perfume," says Frankie.

Ralph takes the money and Frankie goes to the table and sits down with the guys. Everything's back to normal. "I see my Tanqueray on the rocks, thanks Corky. I really mean it, thanks for everything!" They shake hands and hug each other.

Junior says, "Not for nothin', but can we eat now? I'm gonna pass out, I'm so hungry!"

Tommy the Waiter comes by. "Ready for another Tanqueray, Mr. B? Anyone else? Mike wants to buy you all a drink."

"Tell him thanks, but we've had enough. I see the busboy has the cart with all our food on it."

Orlando says, "Thank God for busboys!"

....

Early the next morning at *Mike's Junk Yard*, Frankie pulls into the yard and parks. Mike sticks his head out of the small office, "Hey Frankie, c'mon in and have donuts and coffee. I just made some fresh."

"Okay Mike, but Aldo will be here in a few minutes. I wanna crush the car as soon as he gets here."

Frankie enters the junk yard office and Mike pours some coffee, offering donuts. Frankie takes one. "It's no problem, Frankie. Tell him to pull up to the number two machine and in a coupl'a minutes you'll have an iron cube. Frankie, do you take milk or sugar?"

Frankie nods to both and then Mike sees Aldo pulling into the yard. "Here's Aldo now. I'll tell him where to put the car." Mike goes out. "Hey Aldo, I haven't seen you in a long time. Go on in and have some coffee with Frankie. There's donuts, too. I'll take care of the car."

"Thanks Mike."

Aldo goes into the office. He and Frankie listen as Mike starts the crusher. There are loud crunching noises and then Mike yells, "Here's your iron cube, guys. Come take a look." Frankie and Aldo go out to the crusher and smile.

Frankie says, "Thanks Mike."

Mike says, "For what? You own half the joint!"

....

At *Sing Sing Infirmary and Hospital*, Joe Basilio has been having chest pains and is being checked by a doctor.

"Well Doc, how bad am I? Did I have another heart attack? I feel pretty clammy and it's hard to swallow, ya know, like a piece of bread is stuck in my throat."

"The results of your EKG are not normal, Joe," says Dr. Ashton.

"The pain in your chest is called Angina. The pain you feel radiating down your left arm is another sign of your heart condition. I don't think you've had any serious damage yet, but I'm going to put you on 'light duty'. When you feel a pain, you put this tiny white pill under your tongue. It's a Nitroglycerine pill. And no stress, Joe, understand? I want you to take it easy."

"Thanks Doc, I'll try, but you know around here it's tough."

An Orderly comes into the room and speaking to his friend, Dr. Ashton, says, "Remember that creep, Needles? Guess he messed with the wrong guy up at Folsom. Yep, somebody killed him in the yard in broad daylight. Stuck a steel bar through his ear and right into his brain."

Dr. Ashton replies, "And I bet nobody saw it. No great loss. He was no good."

"He was a bad person all right," says Joe. "I can't say I'm sorry to hear it. Boy, these prisons are sure a dangerous place to live! I gotta get outta here! I gotta get home to my family."

The Orderly and the doctor escort Joe to the entrance to his cell block. The Doctor gives Joe his papers. "Here are your papers for 'light duty', Joe. Now you take care."

"I will Doc, thanks!

....

Aldo and Frankie are at the counter of the *Hollis Diner* in Elmhurst. They're having coffee and talking.

"Aldo, there's gonna be a lot a heat in *Corona* and I'll be the first one they grab. I can handle it, but I want you to go back to Hollywood now."

"Okay Frankie, but you call me if you need me. I really appreciate you lookin' in on my mom too. I'm with ya always, pal."

"My cousin Dickie is meeting in Hollywood next week with a guy named Jerry Strauss. He's gonna put Dickie in a picture they're shootin' in about a month or so. I know they'll want you for the stunts on that film, Aldo. You know, Dickie was nuts about some broad with two kids a while back, but now he's forgot all about her. Now he's got a coupl'a those Hollywood beauties every night of the week."

234

Aldo says, "You just gave me another surprise."

"Yeah, well you told me you like surprises, Aldo. And by the way, I'm really very proud of you. Did I tell you that?"

"Thanks Frankie. You know, my mother don't understand why I can't stay longer. I told her I'm workin' on a picture and I only came back home for your birthday. Frankie, when is your birthday?"

"Same as Columbus so you won't forget. Hey waitress, get us two root beer floats, will ya?"

……………………..

Lou Duro is sitting at his desk in his office. Jack Ecker, Jr. is on the other side of the desk. The men are face to face.

"Jack, we appreciate your interest in seeing the truth come out. If you could get to him, get him to admit to Joe's innocence, that's what we need."

"I know, but he's crazy. He doesn't care."

"I have a signed Affidavit from a lady in Forest Hills who was walking with her son that day. They saw Joe on the passenger side of the car. She said he had his head back and his eyes were closed. Her son even said, *'Mom, is he dead?'* But he was just relaxing. As a witness, she would testify that Joe didn't look like a guy on a robbery."

"I know he's innocent, Lou."

"Even the newspapers think he got a bad deal. So, we've got a break with this lady. It's some help, but not enough Jack."

"I really need to get this nightmare over, Lou! I can't tell you what it's done to my life. It's almost unbearable. It was a good idea making me co-counsel. I can go back day after tomorrow. I'll plead, beg, insult him, whatever I have to do. I guess you know your client Frankie has made it clear what his intentions are?"

"Jack, let's not talk about that. You go and use all your talents and know-how with your father. Get him to sign an Affidavit and I can take it to the governor."

"Don't call that lousy so-and-so my 'father'".

"I'm sorry, Jack. If you can do it, if it works out well, I'll be at the governor's office to get Joe exonerated."

"'If', if is a big word, Lou."

....

Frankie and Corky are watching a television News Broadcast in the parlor of Frankie's house. The TV Newsman is reporting:

> "*It's been a week since the murder of Judge H. Becker who was found shot to death in his flooded driveway. Police are gathering all of the evidence. $2000 in counterfeit money and two bags of cocaine were found among his clothes. Was the judge involved in rackets? Was this a set-up? Was it a Contract Murder? Those questions and many others remain unanswered tonight. No murder weapon has been found and the police are keeping quiet about the case. It appears that the police have their work cut out for them.*"

"Corky, I know you spoke to Orlando and Junior at the *Nook*. But did you convince that kid 'Tommy the Waiter' that I was in the Men's Room? His statement is gonna be very important."

"Don't worry Frankie, he saw you. So did Ralph the Manager. We all got there at 10:30, including you."

Changing the subject, Corky says "Frankie, my girl is takin' steam. I'm never around and I won't let her go out alone. She can't leave the house."

"Why not, why not let her go with Angie to the movies? Right now Corky, I got no head for that kind'a shit, my mind is on a million other things."

"C'mon Frankie, let's go to the Copa, all four of us. I think Tony Bennett is there. The girls will have fun and we'll do our duty, okay? Call Nick and tell him to save us a table for tomorrow night about 9 pm. We'll go eat Chinks and then see the Show."

"Maybe you're right," says Frankie. "Okay, let's do it!"

....

The *Copa Cabana* is the hottest night club in the city. It's an "outfit" joint and Artie "The Sheik" runs the place for the owners who never come in. Nick Kealy is the maitre d`. Nick is 45-50 years old and his real name is not "Kealy" – he's Italian and rumor has it that he's the brother-in-law of crime boss Frank Costello. Anything Nick Kealy wants in New York, he gets. He makes big money as a greeter at the *Copa* because everybody knows him and knows who he is. Frankie goes in three to four times a week and every time he gives Nick a $50 bill.

Corky and Frankie are at the *Copa* with their girls and a couple of guys from Harlem, a couple of guys from Midtown and their guys from Corona. Tony Bennett is appearing and the place is packed. The line of people out front waiting to get in runs all the way down the block. Frankie and his people go in through the back door.

Nick spots them and tells the waiters, "Hey, make room in the middle for Frankie." The show is going on, but the waiters push the tables of patrons aside and set-up tables and chairs in the center of the room.

With Frankie is "Little Corporal", the big boss in Harlem. He's a little guy in a wheel chair and what he says in Uptown New York goes, no discussion. He and Frankie are very good friends and buy their new Cadillac's together every year at the dealership on Broadway. Everybody in the place is a wise guy and, if the F.B.I. walked in, they'd all go to jail.

World Middle Weight Boxing Champ, Carmen Basilio (no relation to Frankie), is a tough kid, a good guy and everyone likes him. He sees Frankie and comes over to his table. "Hey kid, how you doin'? You doin' okay, Frankie?"

"Yeah Carmen, I'm doin' good. How you doin'? Good to see ya." "I want you to meet somebody."

"Who?" Frankie asks

"You wanna meet Sinatra?"

"Geez, yeah I'd like to meet him."

"He'll be happy to meet you, Frankie. Ya know, he doesn't like too many people, but I know he's gonna like you. I'm gonna go tell him about you before I bring you over, okay Frankie?"

"Yeah, sure," says Frankie.

Sinatra is sitting in a big booth with Jilly Rizzo, his bodyguard and lifelong friend, and his whole entourage. They're drinking and laughing and Carmen goes over and speaks to Frank. He comes back and says, "C'mon with me, Frankie." He takes Frankie by the hand and leads him over to Sinatra's booth. He says, "Frank, this kid is a good kid and I want you to meet him."

Frankie says, "Hello Mr. Sinatra, geez I'm so happy to meet you."

"You're a nice looking kid. How old are you?"

"I'm 22, Mr. Sinatra."

"Sit down. Frank is my name."

Frank and Frankie have drinks often and over the next nearly fifty years spend many long nights together into the wee small hours of the morning.

....

Again, Jack Eckers is sent to see Peppers. During the next year, Jack makes three more attempts with Peppers refusing to see him each time. This is Jack's fifth attempt and he is getting weary. He arrives at *Denamora* and is waiting for the guard to come out and tell him once again that Peppers won't see him. To his surprise, he walks into the visiting room. Jack stumbles for words.

"Uh, hello Peppers. Uh, thank you for seeing me. I've been trying to see you for so long, almost a year. I'm in a precarious position and I know you, you're saying, 'What do I care?' But I hope you do care because, to be honest, if you don't sign an Affidavit saying that Joe Basilio is innocent, like I said before, you'll have my death on your hands too."

Trying to hold back his emotions, Peppers says, "You say you're my son. Well, it's true I put you in a Catholic Orphanage when you were two years old, not because I wanted to, but because it was better for you. Your mother was a whore and I beat her up and sent her back to the whorehouse where she came from. I couldn't take care of you. I wanted to see you grow up, but it wasn't in the books."

"I never knew any parents except my mother and father who raised me. Now I'm begging you, please, give Joe his freedom and let me have my life!"

"You were 'little Johnnie' then. At least I saw you again before I die. I wanna call you Son just once, just to see how it feels. Joe has known that feeling all his life. He has a nice wife and kids. I was jealous. I had no one 'til you came back, a little late but . . ."

"Even though I don't know you," says Jack, "I feel this ache in my heart. I know it sounds weird, but I'm talking to a stranger who is my flesh and blood."

"Jack . . . Son . . . Go see the warden, Mr. Lawyer. I'll sign whatever you need me to sign." Looking at his son, Peppers feels a sense of pride.

Suddenly, Jack bursts into tears. "I don't know what to say or how to thank you. Maybe like the kids say, I'll just say, 'Thanks Dad'".

....

Jack drives to *Corona* to see Lou Duro. Lou's secretary, Sue, is a pleasant, attractive and well-dressed Brunette.

"Hi Mr.Ecker. Mr. Duro is in a meeting with Mr. Basilio and he is expecting you. Just a moment please." She pushes a button on her phone and says, "Lou, Mr. Ecker is here to see you." There is a pause and she says, "Go right in, Mr. Ecker."

Jack shakes hands with Lou and Frankie. There is clearly anxiety on both their faces.

Jack is so excited he's ready to jump up and down. He yells out, "We did it! I can't believe it, but we did it! He was so nice . . ."

Frankie and Lou and Jack all jump up together, shaking hands and patting each other on the back. They are overwhelmed with happiness.

Frankie says, "Jesus, Jack, I'm so proud of you. And Lou, man I can't believe you did it, both of you! He caught a beatin' and still he wouldn't crack. What a job you guys did!"

"He admitted that I was his son. He signed everything we need."

"Shit man," says Lou. "This is great, and I have the Affidavit from the lady too!"

Frankie says, "I'll get a letter from the whole neighborhood on Pops character asking the governor to exonerate him. I can't tell you how I feel! C'mon you guys, let me buy you lunch. This is more than a celebration!" Frankie is so choked up he can hardly speak. "This is freedom for my Papa!!"

"Okay Frankie, calm down now. Let's take it one step at a time," says Lou. "First I'll contact the warden and give him a copy of the Affidavit. That'll get the ball rolling."

"Lou, as Co-Counsel, I'll go with you when you get the appointment to see the Governor."

"Sure, Jack," says Lou.

"I gotta call home and tell Mom and Gramma! Then I'm gonna throw a party for all our friends! When

Papa gets home, you'll think it's the Fourth of July or somethin'!"

"Frankie, one step at a time," Lou tells him.

....

Lou Duro and Jack Ecker, Jr. are waiting to see the warden at *Sing Sing.* They're in a waiting area with a small TV. The news is on and both men are listening intently.

> *"It's been over a year now since the murder of Judge H. Becker. Still no arrests have been made. The police have no clues, but they do continue to question members of the Corona Dukes led by Frank Basilio. Police Chief Flannery informed me that they are also questioning drug peddlers and known counterfeiters regarding the counterfeit money that was found in the judge's bedroom the night of his murder. The Chief states that his department is working hard to find new clues and solve this murder. . . now to other news-"*

As Lou Duro gets up to change the TV channel, the warden opens his office door and motions for the men to come in.

Lou says, "Warden, thank you for seeing us. We sure appreciate your cooperation and your letter to the governor on behalf of Joe Basilio. You know Jack here."

"Sure, I know Jack. And it's my pleasure to help Joe. He's a sick man and he was dealt an injustice. I don't know anyone who isn't happy for him. We all want him to spend his remaining years with his family. You know, I've received more than 300 letters from the neighborhood where Joe lived. And thanks to you, Jack, we have the signed Affidavit and confession from John Peppers Graziadei."

"How long do you think it will take for the governor to exonerate him?" asks Lou.

"It shouldn't take more than a week or two at the most. It's just a matter of paperwork. Jack, Peppers was like a changed man when I spoke with him yesterday. He really wants to do the right thing. He said, "For my son.""

"Yes, it's a miracle," says Jack.

"Well Warden, we won't take any more of your time. Thanks again. We'll be in touch." The men shake hands and Lou and Jack leave the warden's office.

....

Ten days later, Lou Duro, Frankie and Jack Ecker, Jr. are sitting in Lou's office reading the headlines:

"GOVERNOR ANDREW GIVENS EXONERATES INNOCENT MAN"

Frankie throws the paper in the air and the three of them jump up with "high fives" all around.

………………………..

It's another routine day at *Sing Sing* except that Joe Basilio is in the yard saying goodbye to his friends. It is an amazing day for the prison too with Joe getting hugs from the Mexicans, the blacks, the whites and his best friend and cell mate, Cornel the Chinaman. Everyone is wishing him "Good Luck" and telling him, "You're a good Wop".

Vito Carulia walks over to Joe. "Mr. Joe, my name is Vito. I know you from before. I told you not to worry about nothin'. You go home now and say hello to your son, Frankie, for me. Tell him I hope he is happy about everything."

"Since you first talked to me in the yard and told me, 'Don't worry about nothin'', I wondered could you be the Angel on my shoulder my son told me about?"

"I'm no Angel, I'm just a Paisano. Now you go home. Goodbye Paisano."

....

The street in front of the prison is jammed with family and friends and newspaper guys. The gate opens and out comes a thin graying Italian man. He is all smiles. He's almost crushed by Gramma and Connie, Uncle Pete, Frankie, Joey, Petey, Corky, all the *Corona Dukes* and many other friends and well-wishers.

Joe is filled with emotion. He lifts his hands up to the sky with tears streaming down his smiling face, "My God, I'm free!!!"

Aldo gets out of his car with two flags, one Italian and one American. He waves both flags and yells, "Papa Joe, we're goin' home!"

Gramma is laughing and crying, "Filia Me!!"

Connie, Frankie and Uncle Pete whisk Joe into Frankie's Caddy and eight cars full of people follow them to Frankie's house.

The house is lit up like a Christmas tree. There are tables of food, wine and beer and a big sign reading:

"WELCOME HOME PAPA JOE"

Outside across the street are two cop cars. They're watching and taking pictures. Frankie and Corky are in the yard and spot them.

"Hey Corky, look across the street. Let's call 'em over to join the party. I bet they never ate food this good in their life! If it wasn't for diners, they'd starve to death!" Both men laugh.

Corky says, "I got two words for them and it ain't 'Happy Birthday'. C'mon, let's hang out with Papa Joe." Corky waves at the cops and grabs Frankie by the arm. They go in the house and Frankie says to Corky, "Remember the game we played when we were kids, Cork? – 'Catch Me If You Can.' They both laugh.

CHAPTER EIGHT

Camilio's Lounge is owned by Antonio Camilio. Antonio owes Frankie and his people a lot of money from gambling and horses. Frankie likes him a lot and doesn't want to strong arm him, but Big Frank tells him, "Frankie, get the money, that's what you gotta do. That's the job we got. We don't get the money, we don't have nothin'."

"Yeah, boss, I know, but I like the guy."

"Okay, Frankie, tell him to give us a piece'a that Lounge he's got. Take the guys Lounge, that's all. What the hell's the difference?"

Frankie and Corky go to talk to Antonio Camilio. Corky says, "Antonio, you know you owe us a lot'a money. You like to gamble and you lost. You gotta pay us back. That's the business we're in."

Frankie says, "I talked to my guy and you know who I'm talkin' about. Look, you know I don't wanna muscle ya because I really think the world of you, so how bout we make a deal for Camilio's? You owe a little money on the joint. We'll accept the debt for whatever you owe and we'll take it over. The equity in the club will cover whatever you owe us."

"Frankie, you and your people have been so good to me and I'm glad you're not gonna do nothin'. I'll be happy to get the hell outta this business anyway. I got so many people that owe me money, I'll never collect. I'll go to the lawyer's office in the morning and sign the place over to you."

Frankie says, "Okay, that's fine, Antonio."

Frankie and Corky are running Camilio's with Big Frank as the "silent partner". Frankie hires a kid by the name of Dominic and puts him to work as a bartender. Dominic is a nice kid - looks like Kirk Douglas. After his first week on the job, he tells Frankie, "Mr. B, I can't thank you enough for the opportunity. You don't know how much money I made!" He takes out a hundred dollar bill and says, "Look, this is the first $100 I've ever earned!"

Frankie says, "Lemme see that," and he takes the hundred dollar bill, tears it in half and throws it on the floor. "Ah, that's nothin', Dominic." The kid looks like he's going to have a heart attack, and Frankie says, "Here kid," and reaches in his pocket, pulls out a wad of money and gives him another hundred dollar bill. "Ya know, the money's still good, Dominic. All you gotta do is tape it back to together." They both start laughing.

Camilio's is a wise guy hangout. Nobody pays. Frankie and Corky comp everybody and at the end of the week Dominic says, "Hey Mr. B, you owe $250."

Frankie says, "But I own the joint."

"Yeah, but you gotta pay for all the comps you gave. And Corky owes even more."

"Ah shit, what are we doin' here?" They both laugh.

....

On his way to collect the vig from a big Broadway producer, Frankie walks into the plush offices of Leo Zuckerman and is greeted by a secretary.

"Welcome to Zuckerman Productions, sir. Do you have an appointment?"

"Hey sweetheart, tell Leo that Frankie's here and wants to see him. He's expecting me."

The secretary pushes a button on the intercom, telling Mr. Zuckerman that Frankie is here. She listens a moment and says, "You can go right in, sir."

Leo is a well-dressed, short, bald guy. He has a cigar in his mouth. Turning to Frankie he says, "Hey Frankie, come on in. How are you? Have a drink."

"Leo, whadya wanna do? You owe $11,000 without the vig. I can't carry you no more. Today is Monday. I'll give ya to Friday for the money. You bring it to Camillio's at 9pm . . . Leo, those horses are gonna get you killed someday."

"Well Frankie, suppose I can't get it by Friday? That's a chunk'a cash and I got a lot invested in a new play."

"Leo, don't talk like a sucker. Have all the cash by Friday night or we collect it from your widow."

....

It's Friday night and *Camillio's Lounge* is filled with well-dressed men and women dancing, drinking and having a good time. Leo enters with Marti, a tall, slender sophisticated lady wearing a mink coat. Handing the maitre d` a $20 tip, he asks him, "Can you give us a booth please and ask Frankie to join us."

"Leo, this is so exciting – meeting a real live hoodlum! But I have to admit that I'm a little frightened at the looks of some of these men in here. I am glad though that I loaned you the money or I'd never get to see a place like this!"

The waiter comes over to take their order and says, "Sir, you are the guests of Mr. Frank Basilio tonight. May I take your order?" Leo and Marti order drinks and as the waiter leaves Leo whispers, "He's a classy bastard, but don't cross him. They're all like that."

Frankie approaches the table and says, "Hey Leo, you're right on time." He looks at Marti and says, "My name is Frank Basilio, how are you?"

"Frankie, this is Mrs. Martha Baron. She is an actress and a producer and she wanted to meet you."

Marti asks, "Would you be angry if I ask you a question?"

Looking at Leo, Frankie says, "She's not a cop, is she?" Frankie smiles and tells Marti, "No, I won't get angry, go ahead."

Marti asks, "Are you a real gangster? I mean, do you do illegal things for a living?"

"Is that supposed to be a joke, lady? Leo, did you bring this broad here so she could see how the monkeys in the zoo live?"

"Sorry Frankie, please don't get upset! She didn't mean any offense."

"I really didn't, Mr. Basilio. It's just that in my whole life I've never met a man like you before".

Frankie turns to Leo. "Come into the office and let's finish our business. Excuse us a minute, Mrs. Baron."

....

A week later, Marti calls *Camillio's.* "Hello, is Frank Basilio in, please."

"Yeah, he's here. Who's callin'?"

"Please tell him that Martha Baron is on the phone for him."

"Hold on a minute, lady."

After a few minutes, Frankie picks up the phone. "Hello Marti. I didn't expect to hear from you."

"Well Frankie, I feel badly about how I behaved the other night. I'm afraid that I offended you and I really didn't mean any harm. It's just that I'd never met anyone like you before. I hope you will let me make it up to you."

"Whadya got in mind, Marti?"

"Do you want to meet me for a drink?"

"Yeah sure, Marti, I'll have a drink with you."

And so it begins . . .

....

Pulling up to the entrance of *Sutton Terrace*, a very swanky building in Manhattan, the doorman greets Frankie. "Good evening, sir. I'll take the car."

"Sure thanks," says Frankie.

He enters the building, but is stopped by a man dressed in what looks like a general's uniform. "Sir, are you a guest of someone in the building? I'm afraid you can't go up until I verify who you are."

Frankie, dressed in a tan trench coat and a 3 inch fedora and looking every inch like what he is, says, "C'mere you. Who the frig are you, some

General of the Army or somethin'? You call the Penthouse, Suite 12K, and you'll find out who I am."

The General calls the Penthouse. "Are you expecting a man dressed . . . I mean, he looks like-" . . . pause . . . "okay, yes ma'am, I'll do that." The General turns to Frankie, "I'm sorry, sir! The lady said for me to send you right up. The elevator is right there, sir."

"I know where the fuckin' elevator is. What are you, new here or somethin'? You should be overseas in the war."

Frankie goes up and rings the bell to Penthouse 12K. An elegant lady opens the door. She is tall and slender with blond hair and brown eyes and appears to be about 15 years older than Frankie. He has learned that her family came over on the Mayflower and settled in Connecticut. Her Aunt is the owner of a large National Paint Factory and her family owns a popular Shoe Manufacturing Company. They are bluebloods and multi-millionaires.

Marti greets him dressed in a stunning house coat. "Oh darling, please come in! I am so sorry they had to verify your entrance. It will never happen again, I promise you. How dreadful for you, darling!"

"I guess I don't look like the blueblood guys with the brown and white shoes and the seersucker suits."

Laughing, Marti says, "No darling you don't, thank God! Come, let's have a martini." She calls the maid. "Ethel, please get us two martini's with olives." Frankie and Marti embrace and kiss with passion. Ethel comes back with the martini's and says, "Hi, Mr. Frank. I am always happy to see you. Miss Martha, he is The Man!" Ethel puts the drinks and hors d'oeuvres down on the coffee table then hurries back to the kitchen.

Toasting, Marti says, "Darling, you really rate high with Ethel, and she doesn't like many people. She especially doesn't like my stuffy friends, you know." She's been with our family for over 30 years, and she's not just a servant, she's my friend too."

"Honey, I came over tonight just to give you a kiss and to say goodbye. I know you want me to stay the night, but I can't tonight. In my business, I can win a lot and I can lose a lot. This week I had a bad streak. I got a serious problem and I gotta go to

258

Florida and see some people. I screwed up some important money and I gotta answer for it."

"What are you saying, Frankie, you 'got to answer for it'? Are you saying you could get hurt or even worse?"

"That's what I'm sayin', sweetheart. But it's not your problem. It's my problem."

"Now you listen to me, Frankie. Your problems ARE my problems. Don't you know that by now? Darling, what does this entail and how much money are we talking about?"

"I'm not gonna get you involved, Marti. This is not the movies. If I don't come up with forty grand, they'll be playin' marbles with my eyes. Do you understand? I gotta go. I'm sorry darling and I hope I'll see you again."

"Dammit Frankie, we'll pay them off. I'll get the money for you from the bank tomorrow and you can pay whoever by 3 o'clock."

"Marti, I don't want your money. I'll handle it."

"What good is money darling if I can't do what I want with it? It's our life together that counts. I

259

love you, Frankie! You stay here with me tonight. No more talk or questions about business. It's settled."

Calling to Ethel Martha says, "Ethel, please put some fillets on the fire with sliced tomatoes the way Frankie likes. And don't forget the Italian bread we found today. Oh, and another round of martini's, please."

Frankie says, "Honey, are you sure it's no problem?"

"It's no problem, but come here! I've missed you terribly!! They settle down for the night, watching the stock market on TV."

....

Frankie's relationship with Marti continues for several years with Marti often encouraging him to get into another line of work. She tells him, "Darling, why don't you just retire and we'll buy a house in the Islands and we can be together all of the time?"

"Babe, you know I'm crazy about ya, but I got stuff I wanna do."

....

Frankie's family is always telling him how handsome he is. Gramma says, "Oh Frankie, you are so handsome, you could be a movie star." Mom says, "Frankie, you should be a singer."

"But, Mom, I can't sing."

"Yes you can, I hear you singing all the time."

"Mom, I'm tellin' ya, I got the worst singing voice in the world."

After coming back from the army, Frankie learned that the G.I. Bill is available to him and he decides that he wants to use it. He is introduced to Anthony Pirella who is a Drama and Vocal coach and has a studio in Manhattan. Mr. Pirella is a good guy, a "legitimate" Italian, and a good coach. Frankie says to him, "Listen, Mr. Pirella, I'd like to become a singer."

"Okay great, Frankie."

"I'm a Vet and I wanna use the G.I. Bill. I sang before I went in the army which interrupted my singing career." (This is what he has to say in order to qualify to use the G.I. Bill.)

"Okay Frankie, this here is Ray, my piano player. Why don't you sing something and Ray will accompany you on the piano." He turns and walks out of the studio.

Frankie says, "Hey Ray, my name is Frankie Basilio."

"Whadya gonna sing, Mr. Frankie?"

"I'll sing 'Maybe You'll Be There'."

"Okay, what key?"

"Uh, any key," says Frankie.

"Any key?"

"Yeah, anything."

Ray looks puzzled, but shrugs and says, "Okay, I'll do an arpeggio and I'll follow you."

Frankie knows about an "arpeggio" like he knows about the man on the moon. Ray starts playing and Frankie starts singing. Ray keeps looking at Frankie. He finishes playing and Frankie still has half the song left. Ray says, "Are you sure you were a singer, Mr. Frankie?"

"Yeah," says Frankie.

"Well, are you mentally okay?" asks Ray.

"Yeah, I'm okay."

"Well, you're not really a singer. You can't sing."

Frankie laughs, and Anthony Pirella comes into the room and says, "Can I see you for a minute, Frankie?" "Sure Mr. Pirella."

"Frankie, I was listening to you sing and I'll tell you the truth. You better find something else to do because you definitely can't sing."

Frankie says, "Yeah I know, you're right, but my mother thinks I'm good."

"Have you ever thought about acting? You could train here. You're a nice looking guy, let's see if you have any acting ability. What do you say to that, Frankie?"

"Sounds good, Mr. Pirella."

"Okay Frankie, you come back on Wednesday at 10 AM." "Okay, and thanks. See ya Wednesday."

Frankie shows up at the studio on Wednesday and he's told that the Drama class is going to do improvisations. Frankie says, "What? Improvisations, what's that?"

"You know, when you ad lib, make up something, make-up a scene."

Frankie is thinking, "Yeah, I can do that."

One of the Drama teachers is a Jewish guy with glasses. He says, "Frankie, you do an improvisation scene with Arnold."

Now Frankie has never been short on words, and he's on the stage with Arnold doing a scene and just making stuff up. The teacher stops them after a few minutes and walks up to Frankie and says, "You know you're very lackadaisical."

Frankie grabs the guy by his tie and says, "What the fuck did you say? What did you call me?"

"Whoa, whoa, whadya doin'? I just said 'lackadaisical', I didn't say a bad word. It just means you're lazy."

"Well then why didn't you just say that?"

"Man, you were ready to strike," says the teacher.

Anthony Pirella has been watching and he says, "Okay Frankie, just relax. I want you to continue the scene but with more emphasis – put some feeling into it."

Frankie continues with the improve scene and at the end of the class Mr. Pirella tells him, "Frankie, you can act. You're a natural."

Frankie continues with acting lessons over the course of the next year and lands stage roles in Arthur Miller's, "*A View From The Bridge*" and Arthur Laurent's' play, "*Home Of The Brave*". At night after the shows, the cast goes to the Automat and Frankie comps everybody since he has more money than any of them. They're all starving actors struggling to pay their rents. Frankie says, "C'mon, have some drinks, sandwiches, coffee, whatever you want, it's on me."

………………………..

Olga is a famous Latin dancer in New York City with two Dance studios. She is much older than Frankie, but she likes him and he likes her. Frankie doesn't know how to dance, but she says, "C'mon Frankie, come on the floor, I teach you to dance."

"Get the fuck outta here. I'm not a fag and I don't like dancing."

She is married to a guy named Pedro, but she tells Frankie, "If you stay with me, I give you one of my studios. You could run it – be the boss."

"Nah, I don't like that fag shit."

"No, no Frankie, it is very good. You could make money."

When Olga is dressed up, she's a sexy looking broad. Everybody notices her. She and Frankie are out late and end up getting a room at the Warwick Hotel. It's late morning when Frankie wakes up, not sure for a minute where he is. He looks on the other side of the bed and sees Olga lying there. She scares the shit out of him! With no makeup on and no eyebrows, she looks like the wrestler, *The Swedish Angel*. She looks so ugly that Frankie can't get out of there quickly enough. He throws on his clothes and tells her, "I gotta go sweetheart," and runs out the door.

....

In the early 1950's, Estes Kefauver is heading a U.S. Senate Committee investigating organized crime. Hearings are being held in fourteen cities with testimony from over 600 witnesses, many of whom are high-profile crime bosses. The Hearings, which are being televised live just as many Americans are buying their first television sets, are making Kefauver nationally famous and introducing many Americans for the first time to the concept of a criminal organization known as the Mafia.

New York City, with five major crime "families", is America's capital of organized crime. Big Frank calls a meeting of his guys. "There's a rat bastard in town by the name of Kefauver who wants to make a name for himself. We're gonna close shop for a while until this Kefauver shit blows over."

After the meeting, Frankie pulls Big Frank aside. "I'm thinkin' of goin' out to Hollywood to be an actor in the movies."

"Yeah, I'd do that if I was you, Frankie. I got connections with people out on the West Coast and I can get ya set up out there."

....

Frankie is thinking about his life and the changes that he wants to make. He's talking with Corky and says, "Ya know, Cork, when I'm talkin' with the old Italian guys in the park, I love to talk Italian to 'em. They laugh and get a big kick out it. They pinch my cheek and say, *'Hey c'mere, Sonny, sit down.'* Discussing stuff with these old timers, I can hear in their voices the anger and the bitterness. It's there. They were bred with it and they brought the Italian heritage over. They came from Italy and a life of poverty. Nobody escaped. People had nothin'. They got to America and were just like all the others suckers on the subway. They came for a new life, but the new life wasn't so 'new'. There was no 'gold in the street' so they brought their dissatisfactions with them and the same inability to get along with each other. They were the same as they always were, only in a different climate, a different country."

Corky says, "Yeah, I know Frankie."

"With Italians, it's always the same. We're always worried about what the other guy's got, how much he's got and how come we don't got it. I admire the Jewish people, I really do, Corky. You gotta give 'em credit. They're a small group of people. And look how many have tried to eliminate them: They were fed to the lions. Germany killed millions. I mean everything happened to those poor people. Just like the Italian immigrants to America, the Jewish people started with nothin', but what they had was a unity. When Saul or Herman or Isaac came from wherever, there'd be a spot for him in a machine shop, a tailor shop or a store. They united. They'd say, '*Bring him to work, don't worry, we'll take care of him and his family.*' Most Italians don't do that. We're good to each other as long as we can get something from each other, but once somebody surpasses somebody else, there isn't so much as a pat on the back. It's, '*That sonovabitch! Look what he did. How'd he get there? Why shouldn't I be there?*' It's a resentment that Italians have. Italians usually don't help each other, Corky."

"Hey Frankie, we help each other."

"Yeah, Cork, but that's different. I'm talkin' generally."

"When you think about culture, the Italians surpass in almost everything: In music, art, medicine. The thing that ruins Italians is ourselves. We blame everybody else if we don't achieve greatness. That's why the 'mobs' got started. Italian-Americans saw the handwriting on the wall and realized that we had to stay close together and take advantage of everybody. The problem is, we take advantage of each other. We prey on our own people. The Jews are different - they borrow from other people to help each other – not shoot each other."

"I know it sounds like I'm knockin' Italians, but I'm not, Corky. I love what I am. But in reality, there's a good and bad side to everything. The Italian family lives more in 'tradition' than in 'reality'. I don't know about everybody else, Corky. I only know how Italian people are 'cause that's all I've ever known. Until I got to a certain age, I thought there was nobody else. There was only Italians, and the rest were Americans, know what I mean, Cork?"

"Yeah Frankie, I know what ya mean. It's the same for me."

"Us New York guys – we're the kinda guys that find our footing right away. We're clever, we're thieves and hustlers and we know the streets 'cause we were raised in the streets and we know all the moves. I think us Italian guys got a certain charisma that people like, ya know?"

"Yeah, a 'charisma' Frankie, that's what we got." They both laugh.

"No really, Corky, us Italian guys got a certain magnetism. I guess other people have it too, but I don't know them. I only know us. . . well, anyway, Corky, I'm gonna go out to Hollywood and become an actor and change my life."

"Well, don't forget about your friends when you're rich and famous, Frankie."

"Never happen, Cork. We'll always be together..."

CHAPTER NINE

A dancer by the name of Grace Betta works in one of Olga's studios. She likes Frankie a lot and he thinks she's real cute. Frankie is leaving for Hollywood and wants company on the long drive.

"Hey Grace, how about you go with me out to Hollywood?" "You mean it, Frankie?"

"Yeah, sure."

"Okay Frankie, I'll go with you, but can I bring my girlfriend Marie us."

"Sure, why not."

Frankie's mom says, "Sonny, don't you eat any of that food on the road. All that stuff is garbage and you don't know what you're gettin'." According to Frankie's mom, any food outside of the neighborhood is bad. She buys a huge provolone on a rope, two huge salami's, two hams, an enormous jar of peppers and several loaves of Italian bread and tells Frankie, "Put this in your car and that way you'll have something good to eat." Frankie is driving his brand new Cadillac Deville. It's powder blue with a white top. He goes to pick-up Grace and Marie in Brooklyn.

"Hey Grace, you ready to go?"

"Oh, yes, Frankie! Ooooh, your car is so beautiful! Will you help me with my suitcase, Frankie?"

Frankie puts the suitcase in the trunk of the car and Grace opens the door, sniffs and says, "What's that smell?"

"Just get in the car. Where's Marie?" Just then, Marie comes down the stairs.

"Hey Frankie, your car is really pretty." She opens the car door, sniffs and says, "What is that awful smell?"

"Just get in the fuckin' car! It's provolone and salami."

The girls are sitting in the car with the windows open, waving goodbye to their mothers who have their heads out the window of Grace's apartment. Grace says, "Frankie, my God, it smells so bad in here."

"Will you just shut up and cut the provolone – make a sandwich."

After the second day on the road, they get used to the smell. They stop at roadside Rest Areas all the way to California and that's all they eat the whole way.

At night, they stop at a motel to sleep. Frankie sleeps with Grace and Marie sleeps on the other side, away from Frankie. For some reason, Marie starts getting jealous of Grace even though they're all supposed to be just friends. The girls start bickering and arguing and if they're not arguing then they stop talking to each other all together. Frankie's had it with them. He pulls off the side of the road, somewhere in Illinois he thinks, gets out of the car and tells them, "Get out!" They get out of the car. "You girls gotta stop this fuckin' arguing! You're drivin' me crazy! I can't stand it!" Frankie takes out his gun and fires it. *Pow! Pow! Pow!* "I swear I'll make ya both walk back to New York!"

Trembling, Marie says, "Oh Frankie, I'm sorry."

Grace says, "Please don't be mad, Frankie. We're sorry. We won't argue anymore."

When they get to Los Angeles, Frankie and the girls get an apartment on Dorchester Street in the middle of Hollywood. Grace whines, "Oh Frankie, you're gonna become a famous actor and I'm gonna be all alone."

274

"Ah shit, don't worry about that. You're not gonna be alone."

....

All the starlets and wannabe actors hang out at *Googy's* and *Schwab's* on Sunset Boulevard. Frankie and the girls pull up outside *Googy's* in the powder blue Caddy with the New York plates. Frankie is wearing a black and white checkered, made-to-order suit and his gangster hat. Mostly guys are hanging around outside – guys like Warren Oates and James Gardner – all wannabe actors and they're watching as Frankie gets out of the car. He hears, "Boy oh boy, will ya look at this guy. Gotta be one of those wise-guy Italians." Two guys are sitting on the curb with their car door open. One of them has his arm inside the door of the car and Frankie turns around and instinctively kicks the door, breaking the guy's arm. He's screaming, "Awwwwww."

Frankie says, "You wanna go a little further, pal?" "Awwwwww. I didn't mean anything."

"Ah, just shut up and get the fuck outta here."

In town less than 48 hours and Frankie has already made a name for himself as a tough guy and a hothead.

Grace and Marie stay with Frankie for a few months, but they're hanging on him too tightly and he ends up sending them back home to New York.

....

Big Frank arranged for Frankie to see a mob guy in L.A. named Rocko who gets him in to see the producer, Joe Sheldon. Joe says, "I like the New York accent and I like the way you talk. I might have something for you." He casts Frankie as a mob guy in an episode of the TV Series, *The Untouchables*. Frankie wears his own hat in the episode.

Later, an L.A. wise-guy by the name of Nico comes up to Frankie in *Schwab's* and says, "Hey, Frankie, I got a mink coat. You think you can get rid of it for me?"

"I don't know, Nico, I'm not in the business."

"Look, it's a full-length Black Diamond mink. It goes for $12,000. All I want is $8,000 for the coat. You know a lot of people – all the rich Jews."

"Ah, I'll see what I can do, Nico."

Frankie goes to see Joe Sheldon. Everybody calls him "Mr. Sheldon" but not Frankie. "Hey Joe, listen, would you be interested in a mink coat?" "A mink coat?"

"Yeah, a full-length Black Diamond mink. It goes for $12,000, but you can get it for $8,000."

"I don't know, Frankie, I'll have to ask my wife."

"Geez, why don't you just surprise her? It's brand new and I'll stand behind it."

"Hmmm, $8,000? Will you take less than that?"

"No, the guy wants $8,000. It's a beautiful coat, Joe."

....

Frankie goes back to see Nico. Nico says, "You want the coat?"

Frankie tells him, "I'll give ya $6,000 for it. All I can get is six grand."

"Are you sure you can't get more?"

"No Nico, that's all the guy will pay."

So, Nico gives him the coat and Frankie takes it to Sheldon and says, "Here's the coat, Joe. You got a hell of a buy for $8,000."

Joe looks at the coat and says, "Oh man, what a beautiful coat! Holy shit, my wife will go nuts over this coat." He gives Frankie the $8,000. Frankie puts $2,000 in his pocket and goes back to give Nico his six grand.

....

The following month, Frankie has a small role in a movie about the life of Barney Ross, a World War II hero and champion professional boxer who became addicted to morphine. The movie is called *Monkey On My Back*. Frankie and Barney Ross were friends in New York and Barney likes the tough but tender quality of Frank's personality so he asks Frankie to be in the film about his life. One of the Producers approaches Frankie on the set and says, "I heard you could get me a mink coat."

Frankie says, "Look, I'm not in the coat business. I'm an actor. I don't know nothin' about coats."

"Oh, I heard maybe you had a connection for mink coats." "Nah, sorry buddy."

Frankie has learned quickly that in Hollywood everybody is a rat and he doesn't trust any of them. They'll sell out their own mothers.

....

All the girls are attracted to Frankie and he usually has more than one that he's going out with. The last thing he wants to do is settle down with any one of them. He's at home and hears somebody talking in the hallway of his apartment building. He opens his door to listen. The voice he hears is coming from above and it's new and strange sounding to his ears. As he goes out into the hallway, a girl is coming down the stairs. She has a beautiful, kind face and he is instantly drawn to her.

"Hey, how you doin'? My name is Frankie."

She looks at him and says timidly in the sweetest Southern accent he's ever heard, "Well, hi Frankie. My name is Sue."

"I've never heard an accent like yours. Where do you come from?"

"I'm from Atlanta, Georgia and I came out here to Hollywood to study acting. I also sing."

Frankie's been around the world and seen many beautiful women, but this Southern beauty captivates him. He's got a phone book filled with phone numbers of girls, but he can't stay away from Sue. It's the first time in his life that he's ever felt a jolt of electricity with a girl and for Frankie its love at first sight.

Soon they are seeing each other constantly. Sue is a really talented singer and is doing well in her Drama classes. In Hollywood, Frankie knows that girls like Sue get "special attention" from agents, directors and producers who can't wait for the newest crop of beauties – naïve kids who come to Hollywood to become a "star". They're promised parts and maybe they get a line or two in a picture, but usually they end up waiting tables or they become whores or high class hookers. Some of them get lucky and go back to their home towns and marry nice guys who work hard for a living. They're the lucky ones. Frankie decides that there is not a "For Sale" sign on Sue. They are married in Las Vegas at The Little White Wedding Chapel on Las Vegas Boulevard. Frankie's friend, Big Mike, is the Best Man at the wedding.

Big Mike is a Boss in the L.A. Mob. The New York organization calls the L.A. syndicate, the "Mickey Mouse Club" because they consider it a watered down version of the bigger and more powerful New York Mob and, even though the L.A. guys are "made guys", they don't mean too much to anybody.

Frankie is Godfather to Big Mike's kid and they hang out together in L.A. Big Mike introduces Frankie to Johnny Stompanato, also known as "Handsome Harry" and "Johnny Stomp". Johnny is a former United States Marine and a bodyguard and right hand man to gangster Mickey Cohen. Frankie and Big Mike are hanging out at the Luau in Beverly Hills, a restaurant owned by the husband of Lana Turner.

"Hey Frankie, there's somebody I want ya to meet. Lemme introduce you to Johnny Stompanato. He's a friend'a mine."

"Yeah sure," says Frankie. "I've heard'a him. I'd like to meet him. Johnny Stompanato is at the bar and Frankie and Big Mike walk over to him.

"Hey Johnny, how ya doin'? I wanna introduce you to my friend Frankie here. Frankie is out from New York."

Johnny says, "How you doin' Frankie? Nice to meet you. What are ya doin' out here on the West

Coast? Did you get tired of all that cold weather back there in New York?"

"Yeah, Johnny, I needed a change a climate, know what I mean?" They all laugh.

Frankie and Johnny become good friends. Johnny has a reputation as a gangster with a big dick who's screwed more Hollywood stars than you could count. He's a wannabe actor and is impressed that Frankie is getting acting roles in movies and TV. Johnny is dating Lana Turner and he introduces Frankie to her. Soon, Frankie is running weekly card games out of her house on North Bedford Drive in Beverly Hills.

The famous Hungarian-born actress and socialite, Zsa Zsa Gabor, lives across the street from Lana and Johnny tries to set-up Frankie for a date with her. "Hey Frankie, lemme fix ya up with Zsa Zsa. She's hot for ya."

Zsa Zsa is considerably older than Frankie, but he's always gone for older broads so that doesn't bother him. But Frankie tells him, "Nah, Johnny, I got my girl, ya know, and we haven't been married that long."

....

Frankie and Johnny are at the Mocambo Club on Sunset Boulevard in West Hollywood. The club is a favorite hangout of people in the motion picture business and it's the most popular dance spot in town. They're sitting at a table when Frank Sinatra and Ava Gardner walk in, smiling happily. Sinatra and Ava just got married, and Frankie is thinking, "Ah shit, Johnny used to go out with Ava, Frank is very jealous, this might be bad."

Frankie turns to Johnny and says, "C'mon Johnny, let's get outta here."

Ava spots Johnny and rushes over, "Johnny, how are you?" She hugs and kisses him on the cheek.

Sinatra looks at Johnny and says, "What the fuck are ya doin'?" "I know her from before you," says Johnny.

"Yeah, well stay the fuck away."

Frankie can't say a word because he's friends with both of them, so he just stands there like Mickey The Mope.

Sinatra looks at Frankie and says, "Hey Frankie, how are ya?" Frankie can tell that he's steamin' and wants to pick up a table and throw it at Johnny, but he and Ava just walk away.

Frankie tells Johnny, "Sit down, what's the matter with you?"

Johnny says, "Well, she's a girl I used to go with."

"Geez, Johnny, let's just relax, have our drinks and listen to Frances Faye here on the piano, okay, buddy?"

Frankie is a little upset about the scene with Sinatra, but he's sitting there listening to the music when all of a sudden he feels something hit him in the back of the head. He turns, but doesn't see anything. A few seconds later, he again feels something hit him in the back of the head. It's an ice cube and he hears a girl laughing, "Ha ha ha". Frankie looks behind him and sees a guy sitting between two beautiful broads and they're all laughing. The guy is a short, fat Jew guy with no hair. His name is Jonie Taps and he's a Producer and Studio Executive. He gets up and heads in the direction of the Men's Room. Frankie tells Johnny, "Hey, I gotta go to the Men's Room. I'll be right back."

Johnny says, "Okay, pal."

When Frankie enters, Jonie is standing at the urinal taking a leak. Frankie goes up behind him and slams his face into the wall. Jonie falls into the urinal with blood pouring out of his nose. He's pissed all over himself and is hanging onto the urinal, bleeding. Frankie turns around and walks out. He goes back to the table and says, "C'mon Johnny, let's go home."

"Whadya wanna go for, Frankie? We just got here."

"C'mon, let's pay the check and get outta here."

"Why? What did ya do, Frankie?"

"Nothin', c'mon let's go."

They get up, pay the check and leave with Jonie Taps bleeding all over the floor of the Mocambo Club Men's Room.

....

While filming *The Untouchables* episode, Frankie gets to know Robert Stack who plays Eliot Ness. Stack introduces Frankie to Richard Conte (also an Italian-American) and his wife, actress Ruth Story, and they become very good friends. Ruth says to Frankie, "They're holding auditions for Arthur Miller's play *A View*

From The Bridge at Players Ring Theatre and I think you'd be perfect in it. Why don't you come down and audition?"

"Geez thanks, Ruth, I really appreciate it. I had a part in New York in that play. I'll be sure to go down and audition."

Players Ring Theatre is on Santa Monica Boulevard in West Hollywood. It's a very popular little theatre in-the-round and is considered a leading actor's showcase venue. Every actor in town wants to work there. Frankie works in *A View From The Bridge* production for more than a year with Sue often coming to see the play.

....

In the late 1950's, Frankie is becoming a familiar face on TV, landing minor roles in episodes of *Wagon Train*, *Gunsmoke*, *The Thin Man*, *Playhouse 90*, *Alcoa Theatre* and *The Detective*. He tries valiantly to juggle a legitimate acting career with his other, not so legitimate, interests.

His family back in New York always wants to be near him because they know he will put them in action. His brothers, Joey and Petey, call him. "Gee Frankie, we can't make a buck here in New York. Can we come out to Los Angeles?" So Frankie's brothers come out.

Joey is a tough guy, big and strong, and he knows cars. He meets a guy who has a car lot and becomes partners with him. Petey goes into the restaurant business.

Frankie's good friend, Johnny Stompanato, is in a tumultuous relationship with Lana Turner. Lana's fourteen year old daughter, Cheryl, is living with her in the house on North Bedford Drive where Frankie holds weekly card games. Lana is trying to break off her relationship with Johnny, and he is having none of it. On the evening of Good Friday, April 4, 1958, Johnny and Lana are having yet another argument in Lana's bedroom. They are yelling and fighting with Cheryl listening in the hallway. She hears Stompanato say, *"You'll never get away from me. I'll cut you good, baby. No one will ever look at that pretty face again."* Cheryl goes down to the kitchen and comes back with a 10-inch carving knife. She is pounding on the door begging for them to open the door when Stompanato comes rushing out and collides with the knife that Cheryl is holding. It enters his chest, severing his aorta. His last words are, *"My God, Cheryl, what have you done?"*

....

Frankie and Sue are driving down Wilshire Boulevard and Frankie says, "Sweetheart, I was thinkin' that I'm not makin' that much money with the TV parts and the coupl'a movies I've done so I might make a change. I've gotta shot at bein' the Maitre d' at a new restaurant and I can make some good money and learn the business. Don't forget, Suzy, we got big plans – you and me. You say that Show Biz ain't worth it and I think you're right. But I still think you could be a star!"

"I don't want to be a star anymore, Frankie. My life is different now. You've taught me so much about life and I just want to spend it with you, honey."

....

Dodger Stadium, built into the hillside of the Chavez Ravine valley opens in 1962, providing spectators with a breathtaking view of downtown Los Angeles to the south; green, tree-lined Elysian hills to the north and east; and the San Gabriel Mountains beyond. Four of the five Stadium seating decks stretch from foul pole to foul pole. The top upper deck stretches from the first base side to the third base side. The exclusive, members only Dodger Stadium Club restaurant is noticeable at the end of the first base grandstand. Numerous employees have been hired for this most prestigious club as well as a few

288

"special employees" like Frankie who is installed as Maitre d'. A-List celebrities such as Film Director Frank Capra, Actress Doris Day, Frankie's good friend Frank Sinatra, Actor Dean Martin and his wife Jeanne and sports stars like Sandy Koufax, Joe Pepitone and Don Drysdale all frequent the Stadium club. After the season ending 156 games at Dodger Stadium, Frankie decides it's time for him to retire. He's met such fabulous people and he tells Sue, "I am honored and privileged to have met these people. It's all about the people, Sue. They are all so special to me – all of them."

....

Frankie is running a popular seafood restaurant called Sorentino's in Burbank with his brother, Petey. Frankie has made a big name for himself in Burbank. Nobody messes with him. There's a regular that comes in. His name is Ivan and he's a big guy – about 6 foot 3. Something is not quite right about Ivan. He likes to harass women in the lounge. On this particular night, Ivan comes in and sits down next to some guy's wife. He puts his arm around her and says, "Hello honey." A waitress sees that the woman is uncomfortable and goes to find Frankie. "Frankie, I need your help in the lounge."

"What's the matter, Alice?" "Ivan's causing trouble again."

"Don't worry about it. I'll take care of it."

Frankie walks into the lounge and goes up to Ivan. "C'mere you!"

"What?"

"I said c'mere. I wanna talk to you."

"Nah, I don't wanna get up. If I do, I'll probably crush you."

Frankie grabs him by the throat and pushes his head into the juke box.

"C'mon outside so I can talk to you, okay?"

"Okay, okay."

Frankie gets him outside. They look like Mutt and Jeff. The guy is easily 6 foot 3 and Frankie is 5 foot 9. Ivan takes a swing and misses. He swings wide – like a girl – and Frankie knows he can nail this guy even as big as he is. Frankie hauls off and hits him as hard as he can in the jaw. Ivan goes down and gets right back up smiling.

Frankie's finger is broken on his left hand. Petey comes running outside and Frankie tells him, "Go get me the gun. Right now. Hurry up."

Frankie hits Ivan another shot in the chin – *Bam!* – and Ivan smiles and looks at Frankie like he hasn't a clue what's going on. It's like you can't hurt him. You can't knock him out. Frankie's brother, Joey, happens to be in the restaurant eating and he rushes outside and picks up a big iron pipe. "You dirty rat! You broke my brother's hand! You won't go down, eh? I'll make ya go down." He takes the iron pipe and hits him in the head, splitting his head wide open.

Ivan starts laughing, "Ha ha ha, I'm not finished with you grease balls." He's bleeding like a stuck pig. Frankie hits him again on the other side of his face and knocks him down. They are out in front of the restaurant and Frankie is kicking him. Cars are passing by and people are gawking and watching the spectacle.

A car pulls up to the curb and the driver takes out a gun, pointing it at Frankie. "Leave that man alone. What's wrong with you? You're killin' that guy!"

Frankie walks right up to the car and says, "You wanna die right now, you motherfucker?"

"No, no, please don't do anything! This is only a starter gun. It just fires a blank cartridge. I just thought I could stop the fight."

Frankie gives him a little slap and says, "Get outta here. Go home."

The cops pull up and Ivan is lying on the ground. An Irish cop by the name of Tiny gets out of the patrol car. He's as big as Ivan. "Hey, what the hell are you guys doin' here?" He puts his hand on his gun.

Frankie says, "Whoa, whoa, hold on."

Frankie and the cop start arguing and the cop says, "I'm gonna lock you guys up."

Frankie says, "You gonna lock us up? You better lock the three of us up and you'll be lucky to get to the station."

He looks at Frankie again and says, "I know you."

"Yeah, well I know you too. Why don't you listen to the story? This guy's a psycho. He comes walkin' into the restaurant and attacks me. He pulled out a pipe and tried to hit me with it and I defended myself. My brother Joey here defended himself, too."

"Ah, I'd really like to lock all three of you Dago's up but I'm gonna take this guy with me (indicating Ivan)." Ivan is bleeding all over the place, his head is split wide open and he's kicking and laughing, "Ha ha ha, you think you got me. Don't worry, I'll get you guys." The cops shove him into the patrol car. "We outta take you in too."

"If you take me, you better take my brothers too if you can do it."

The cops snort, get in the car and drive away with Ivan.

....

Frankie keeps an apartment in Burbank where he runs a bookmaking business. The apartment is upstairs on the second floor. Frankie's pal, Jimmy, works in the business with him. They arrive at the apartment building and are going up the stairs when Frankie spots two Irish guys in the hallway and knows instinctively that they're Detectives. "Jimmy, these guys are cops. I think we're gonna get hit right now." As soon as he says this, the door to the apartment comes flying open and is hit so hard that it comes right off the hinges, nearly slamming into Frankie and Jimmy.

"We finally got you!"

"You got no one," says Frankie. They push him down in a chair and a sergeant hits him in the mouth with his gun, knocking a tooth out. When Frankie tries to get up, a black detective puts his gun to Frankie's head and says, "Please move so I could blow your guinea head off." Frankie is mad as hell, but Wayne Newton is singing Danke Schoen on the radio and suddenly there's this moment of comic relief.

Jimmy is an older guy, a nice man with a stutter. He says, "Ffffrankie, ddddon't sssstart no ttttrouble. Ddddon"t hurt the ggguy. Ddddon't ddo nothin'."

"Don't worry, Jimmy, I'm not gonna do nothin'. Let 'em take us to jail. We'll be out in a coupl'a hours."

The cops put Frankie and Jimmy in cuffs and haul them off to jail. Three hours later they let them out.

....

A couple of detectives show up at Sorentino's two days later. "Hey Frankie, we heard you got a smack down from the boss the other day."

Frankie tells them, "Yeah, he's a real tough guy. Do me a favor, will ya? Here's a message for your

Sergeant. You tell him to come down here, take off his badge and his gun, and I'll pull his pants down and fuck him in the ass."

The Sergeant goes to the District Attorney and tells him about Frankie's message. "Listen, I'm getting ready to retire and I don't need this. There's only a certain kind'a guy that uses that particular terminology. I'm worried for me and my family, so I'm gonna pack it in."

After that, there's a police car in front of Frankie's house every day. He opens the door and says, "Hey guys, c'mon in and have some coffee." It makes them angry because he isn't intimidated by them, but he and Sue decide that it's time for a change. She says, "Frankie, you belong in Las Vegas."

CHAPTER TEN

Frankie decides to leave Hollywood and his acting career behind and get back to his New York roots – gambling, loving people and being tough enough to make his way in a strange new city. He makes a promise to Sue that he will sever all Mob ties and go it alone. He and Sue and their kids arrive in Las Vegas nearly penniless. Frankie is driving his old Cadillac when the transmission goes out on Tropicana Boulevard. Joey is following in his car. They leave the Cadillac, pile into Joey's car and drive to the Boulder Highway area looking for a place to stay. It's obvious that the Las Vegas economy is bad. "Foreclosure" signs and boarded-up buildings are everywhere. They find a completed housing development where no one is living and move themselves into one of the houses. Joey shows Frankie how to turn on the water. The dirt on the window sills is an inch thick. There's no furniture.

After a while, one of the owners of the property finds them there. "Hey, what are you people doing here? You can't just move yourselves into a house."

"Look buddy, we got nowhere else to go. The house is empty. Nobody wants this house. When I get on my feet, I'll be happy to pay," Frankie tells him.

"There's something wrong with you."

"Yeah, I'm a little nuts and I'd think nothin' of blowin' your head off. I'll kill ya and leave ya right here, pal."

"Why don't you buy one of these houses? You could get it for $12,000 to $13,000."

"I can't buy a house. I can't even make a rent payment."

The next month, the guy comes by and asks for the rent and Frankie tells him, "I don't have it."

"Well, you gotta get out."

"Please, don't make me threaten you pal because I promise I'll kill ya. This is survival. My wife and kids gotta have a place to sleep."

This goes on for six months with Frankie threatening him the same way every month and telling him to come back again next month. Eventually, the entire development is sold, Frankie gets a job at The Mint as a shill making $8.00 a day and the family moves out.

....

Attorney Oscar Goldman comes to town and opens an office. He sues The Mint on behalf of the workers for overtime that they are not being paid. Workers at The Mint are required to work 48 hours a week, but are only paid for 40 hours. Goldman asks each worker to pay him $25.00 to file the lawsuit. They win the suit and Frankie tells Oscar, "You're my hero. You got me back all this money and got me back on my feet." He is able to move his family into a small house that is in foreclosure and eventually he is able to buy the house.

Frankie finds it tough to adjust to the Las Vegas style of gambling which is very different from the gambling and bookmaking business in New York. He works his way up to occasional Floor Manager.

Leo is an old-timer and a close friend of Benny Banion. He's a short, fat guy and he likes Frankie. It's Christmas and he says, "Frankie, how much you makin' here?"

"I do okay, Leo."

"How's the family? How are the kids?" "Oh, they're fine, Leo. Thanks for askin'."

Leo takes a $50 bill out of his pocket and gives it to Frankie.

"Get outa here, Leo. I don't wanna take money from you."

"Frankie, don't start with me. I want you to take this money and buy the kids some presents for Christmas."

....

Two guys pull-up on Fremont Street in a red Cadillac and come into The Mint asking for Frank Bassilio. You can tell that they aren't Harvard guys. Frankie is pointed out to them and they come over to him and ask, "Hey, are you Frank Bassilio?"

"Yeah, who's askin'?"

"We've been told by Big Jack to drive you to the Desert Inn Casino to go to work."

Big Jack is the Mob Boss out of Cleveland and Frankie once did him a favor. Frankie says, "Guys, please thank Big Jack for me and tell him I really appreciate it, but I'm married now with a family and I really don't want any favors. Tell him no hard feelings."

The next day, Frankie is fired from The Mint. He is told that The Mint received a letter from the L.A. Police Department saying that Frankie was sent to Las Vegas to organize a crew for the Mob.

Leo hears about Frankie being fired, tracks him down and tells him, "Frankie, go across the street to the California Club. My son, Al, runs the place. I've told him about you and you're gonna start working there."

Al is a great guy and tells Frankie, "I'm gonna put you on the craps table."

"But, Al, I don't know nothin' about dealin' craps."

"Don't worry about it. You'll learn. And, you're gonna get a raise. You'll be making $18.00 a day in tokes."

"Holy Geez! But, Al, I don't even know how to deal."

"Don't worry about it. Just think about what you have to pay out and take 10% off that. When you overpay, I'll let you know."

With Al's teaching, Frankie becomes a pretty fair dealer. The Four Queens opens up and Al says,

"Frankie, you got a shot over there. They pay up to $25.00 a day and the tokes are good."

Frankie goes to work at the Four Queens making $40-$50 a day.

....

Sometime later, a friend of Frankie's who is the maitre d' at the Tropicana says, "Frankie, c'mon over here and work as the Lounge Boss." Frankie doesn't really like being a dealer and wants to use his training as a maitre d' so he jumps at the chance.

....

The Las Vegas Culinary Union represents workers in the hospitality industry, including hotels, casinos, airports, food service, restaurants and laundry services. It is a powerful Union whose influence is remarkably important in an economy dominated by a single industry. Culinary Union General Secretary, Al Brantlett, is as powerful a man as Las Vegas has ever seen. He is running for re-election and he approaches Frankie, asking him to get rid of a guy who is running against him in the election. In exchange, Frankie is to receive the much-coveted "Captains Book" which will enable him to go to work in any Hotel in Las Vegas. Two days before Frankie is to see this guy, Al Brantlett calls and says, "Hey Frankie, you know that matter we were discussing?"

"Yeah," says Frankie. "What about it? I was just getting' ready to go see the guy."

"Well look, Frankie, I want you to just forget about it. Okay? You understand?"

"No, I don't understand. You and me, we had a deal. A deal is a deal."

"Sorry Frankie, but the deal's off." And he hangs up the phone.

Frankie gets into his car and drives to the Culinary Union Offices. Al Brantlett's Secretary greets him as he enters. "Hello, may I help you, sir?"

"I'm here to see Al."

"What is your name, sir?"

"I'm Frank Basilio."

"I'm sorry, Mr. Basilio, but Mr. Brantlett is busy now and you do not have an appointment."

Frankie walks past the secretary and into Al Brantlett's office. He sits down next to him, reaches into his pocket, pulls out a gun and puts it right in his face. "Listen Al, I'm not a Vegas pussy who wants'ta be a tough guy, you understand? I'm from New York. We had a deal and I depended on your honor. You broke your promise, and I promise you I'll leave you dead right here and now."

Al turns white as a sheet and says, "Frankie, please, put the gun away. I'll help you." He picks up the phone and makes a call. After a few minutes of conversation, he hangs up and turns to Frankie. "Okay Frankie, you go to Caesar's Palace tomorrow and you start as Captain."

....

At Caesar's Palace, Frankie has his Captain's Book, but he is completely lost. He's in charge of eight Captains and doesn't have a clue what he's doing. He's having coffee with his friend Jasper who is from the old neighborhood in New York. Jasper is also working at Caesar's.

He says, "Frankie, I want you to meet an important guy." They walk into a private dining room and Jasper says, "Hello Jimmy. I'd like you to meet my good friend, Frankie Basilio."

"Frankie, this is Jimmy Hoffa."

"What a pleasure to meet you, Mr. Hoffa."

"Frankie, my friends call me Jimmy. Sit down, have a seat."

"Thank you, but I better not. It won't go over too well with the Hotel brass if I sit down with ya, you know what I mean."

"You're a pretty sharp guy, Frankie. Are you happy here?"

"Well, Jimmy, I been asked to go to the Stardust."

"Yeah, well that's our place too. You let me know if I can

help." "Thanks a lot, Jimmy. I appreciate it."

....

Frankie has to continually live down his past reputation. Detectives regularly come into the places where he's working just to harass him.

"Hey Frankie, how ya doin'?"

"Who's askin'?"

They show him their badges and say, "We just wanna say hi. You keepin' your nose clean, Frankie?" They're sure that Frankie is working for the Mob.

....

When Frankie moves to the Stardust, it's an absolute pleasure to work there. It isn't a "job". Frankie is welcomed with open arms and he feels safe and at home. It's like a family. The attitude is warm and nobody is trying to prove anything. The Stardust has the best Lounge in Vegas with the first circular Lounge that Vegas has ever seen. Continually revolving shows attract all the major Stars. Anybody and everybody who is anybody comes to the Stardust – good guys, bad guys, legitimate guys and not-so-legitimate guys. There's a guy that comes in regularly. He's a little guy. Doesn't dress too sharp. He says, "Hi how ya doin'?"

Frankie says, "Fine, how you doin'?"

"Gee, I'd really like to see the Royal Show Band from Ireland."

"Yeah, sure, c'mon in." Frankie tells the Captain, "Put him up in the front and give him a coupl'a drinks." Frankie doesn't know this guy from a cord of wood and figures he's just some broke guy. He comes in for about a year and a half and Frankie always puts him up front and comps him. Frankie learns that his name is Bob.

....

The Food and Beverage Director at the Stardust is a guy by the name of Kenny Ryan. He and Frankie are friends and hang out together. Technically, Kenny is Frankie's Boss. They're sitting in one of the restaurants at the Hotel and Kenny starts talking about his days in the army onboard a ship. "We were in a terrible typhoon and the ship almost went down."

"Really? Well, it couldn't have been as bad as the typhoon that I was in which just about tore the ship in half. What was the name of the ship you were on?"

"It was the *Aichen Victory*," says Kenny.

"What? You were on the *Aichen Victory*?"

"Yeah."

"Well, I was on the same ship, Kenny."

"You gotta be kiddin' me?"

"No, honest to God, I was there, Kenny. Let me tell you a story you might just remember. Do you remember in the middle of a storm. . ."

"Oh, what a fuckin' storm!"

". . . there was an argument between a big guy and another guy by the name of Anthony. Anthony was a friend of mine and he was afraid of the big guy. The big guy says to Anthony, '*I'm gonna whip your ass.*' So I get up and say, 'If you're gonna whip someone's ass, c'mon I'll take you on and I promise you it'll be your ass gettin whipped.' So there we are in the middle of this raging storm and the ship is swaying back and forth and here's us two guys fightin' down in the hatch."

"Get outta here. That was you?"

"Yeah, I swear that guy was me."

"I remember you guys fightin' and you could hardly hit each other because the ship was rolling so bad and you kept getting' thrown around by the storm."

"Well, Kenny, that was me. And here we are talkin' about it 30 years later! It truly is a small fuckin' world . . ."

Frankie's brother, Petey, calls from L.A. and says, "Frankie, I can't make a buck out here. I wanna come out to Vegas."

"Sure, Petey, come on out. I'll put ya in action."

Frankie calls a guy he knows at the Union. "Hey Louie, my kid brother is comin' out from L.A. Get him a work card, will ya?"

"Okay Frankie, but you know it's really tough to do. Everybody's always watchin'."

"Don't worry about it. Just get him the card," says Frankie.

Petey goes to work in Room Service at the Stardust. Andre, an old timer and a maitre d' in the other Lounge at the Stardust, tells Frankie, "They're gonna open up the new MGM. Why don't you go over there and take one room and I'll give your brother the other room?"

Frankie tells him, "Nah, I'm happy here at the Stardust and anyway I had a fight with one of the owners at the MGM and he doesn't like me too much."

Petey goes to the MGM and becomes Maitre d'.

....

Whenever Sinatra is in town, Frankie seats his last show at the Stardust Lounge, jumps in his car and runs over to Caesar's where Frank is appearing. They hang out together until 5, 6, 7 in the morning. The Lounge is roped off with security everywhere. Paul, the head security guy, says, "Hey Frankie, how are ya? C'mon in." Frankie goes in and Sinatra (like he always does with Frankie) stands up and puts his arms around him. He calls Frankie "Don Cheech". "Hey Don Cheech, how are ya?"

"Hello, Frank. How are you?"

Frankie thinks to himself: *Here I am, a New York hoodlum tryin' to make a livin' in Vegas and here I am in the presence of Frank Sinatra.*

A lot of people don't like Sinatra because they think he's an egotistical guy, but he's a phenomenal guy if he's your friend.

Jilly Rizzo says, "I've lived with this guy. I was raised with him. It's unbelievable some of the things he does for people. Things nobody knows about." He and Jilly were in a taxicab in Paris and it was raining. The front fender of the cab bumped a kid on a bicycle. Frank got all excited and upset. He jumped out of the cab in the rain, picked-up the kid and the kids bicycle and says, "Are you okay, kid?" The kid wasn't hurt, but Frank reaches in his pocket and takes out everything he has (it could have been $100 or $10,000) and puts it in the kids hand and says, "Son, go buy another bicycle." He was soaking wet when he got back into the cab.

The guys are all sitting around a big table in the Galleria Lounge at Caesars waiting for Frank. Jilly tells everyone, "Don't talk to Frank when he comes in. He's had an argument with Barbara." Frank's wife, Barbara, is a wonderful lady, but she can be a hothead. Frank's a hothead, too. He comes into the Lounge after his show. His shirt is open and he sits down. Frankie says, "Frank, how you doin'?"

"I'm so fuckin' aggravated. Bein' married is a pain in the ass, ya know?" Frankie says, "Yeah, you're tellin' me."

Sinatra looks up at the ceiling and says, "It's fuckin' cold in here."

He's just looking for an excuse to let off some steam, but management calls this old guy – he's about 90 – his name is John - and whenever Sinatra is in town

John puts on his tuxedo and hangs around just in case Mr. Sinatra needs anything. John walks over and says, "Hello Mr. S."

Sinatra loves this guy and gives him hundred dollar bills every time he sees him. "John, come here. This fuckin' air conditioner is killing me. I got a bad cold as it is."

"Okay, Mr. S. I'll take care of it."

"Go get the damn air conditioner guy and bring him back here." "Sure thing, Mr. S."

Everybody is just sitting there not saying a word. About ten minutes later, a guy comes in with a really big, tall ladder. He says, "Mr. Sinatra is there something I can do? Is it the air?"

"Yeah, the fuckin' air blowin' on me is killin' me. I've got a cold. Shut the damn thing off."

"Yes sir."

He puts up the ladder, goes up and adjusts the vent. When he comes back down, he says, "Okay sir, I fixed it for you. You won't have no more air blowin' on you."

Sinatra says, "Okay, you can go."

Twenty minutes go by and Sinatra calls John over. "John, come here."

"Yes, Mr. S. What can I do for you?"

"Go get that air conditioner guy. Bring him back here."

"Is something wrong, Mr. S?"

"Just go bring him back here."

Another ten minutes go by and here comes the guy with the ladder again. He stutters and says, "Mr. uh . . . Mr. uh Sinatra, did I do something wrong?"

Sinatra looks at him and says, "Nah, you didn't do nothin' wrong. You did a good job. Here." And he hands him a $100 bill and says, "Go on, put this in your pocket. Go have a drink."

....

Everybody is sitting around talking about the guys they know. Frankie says, "Hey Frank, you remember Pete Brady?" (Pete Brady is not his real name. He's an Italian guy, connected, from

Youngstown, Ohio. He and Frankie work together at the Stardust. They call Pete the Dean Martin of the Crap Pit. He's a Pit Boss and he's a big, tall, good looking tough guy.)

Frank says, "Yeah, I remember him. He used to deal me craps in Florida. Yeah, he's a nice guy."

Frankie says, "Geez, it's a shame, what happened to him."

"What happened to him?"

Frankie says, "He's in the hospital. He's got cancer."

"He's got cancer? How long has he been in the hospital?"   "About two weeks. It doesn't look too good for him."

Sinatra says, "Oh Geez, I'm sorry to hear that."

And that was the end of the conversation.

The next day, Frank's personal assistant, Dorothy, goes to see Frankie and says, "Frankie, I need to ask you a question."

"Sure, what is it, Dorothy?"

"This has to remain very confidential and cannot be spoken of again."

"Yeah, okay, what is it?"

"You told Mr. S. something about Pete Brady being in the hospital and Mr. S. wants to know what hospital he's in, but he doesn't want anyone to know that I even asked you about it."

Frankie says, "Okay, no problem. He's in Sunrise Hospital."

Two days later, Sinatra goes over to Sunrise Hospital and picks up Pete Brady's entire hospital bill - $15,000 – for a guy he hasn't seen in years. This is the kind of guy he is, but by the same token, he thinks nothing of throwing a glass across the room or blowing up at somebody over nothing if he's in a bad mood. He's a moody kind'a guy.

....

Barbara Streisand is performing at the Desert Inn and Frankie gets a comp for her show. He's sitting in the second row from the stage. After the show, Jilly Rizzo spots him and says, "Don Cheech, whadya doin' here?"

"I just saw Streisand's show. How you doin', Jilly?"

"Yeah, well I'm doin' good. But why don't you go see the old man? He's all by himself, sitting at the bar in the Lounge."

Frankie walks into the Lounge and Sinatra is having a drink after just finishing his show at Caesar's. Frank hugs him and says, "Frankie, have a drink."

"Okay, I will."

Sinatra has his usual Jack Daniels and Frankie has a VO on the rocks. Frank has had two or three before that. He says to the girl bartender, "Lemme have a Jack Daniels on the rocks. Nah, just gimme a Jack Daniels straight up." The girl comes back with the drink and Frank says, "What's this? There's no ice in here." She doesn't want to tell him that he asked for it without ice, so she says, "Oh, I'm sorry Mr. Sinatra, I'll put some ice in it."

She puts two ice cubes in the drink and brings it back to him. "Okay, Mr. S?"

He says, "Jesus Christ, this has more ice in it than Alaska." She says, "I'm so sorry, Mr. Sinatra, I'll fix it."

He looks at Frankie and says, "Whadya gonna do, a girl bartender!

....

Frankie is at Caesar's and Barbara Sinatra is there too. Everybody is waiting for Frank's mother to come in from San Diego. She is flying in during a snow storm. Barbara says to Frankie, "Please stay with Frank. He's absolutely a wreck right now because he knows that his mother is on the way and there's a snow storm."

Frankie says, "Sure, Barbara, I'll stay with him."

They go into the Baccarat Room. It's about 5:00 AM. They're all sitting around the table – some wise guys and some of the bosses from Caesar's. Frank is sitting next to Frankie and says, "Jesus Christ, I don't know what's gonna happen. I don't know how I did the show tonight."

Frankie tells him, "Frank, everything's gonna be all right."

They order some food. Frankie orders a cheese sandwich and Frank has a hamburger. They're trying to eat when they get the news that the plane has crashed. Frank almost passes out. Barbara comes back downstairs and Frank puts his head down, weeping. He says, "Gimme another Jack Daniels." He has two or three more drinks in a row and now can barely stand up. Barbara says to Frankie, "Stay with him until you can get him to the private elevator and then bring him up." They continue drinking until about 11:00 AM. Frankie says, "Frank, are you okay?"

He mumbles something incoherent. Frankie says, "C'mon, let's go upstairs."

"Nah, nah I wanna stay here."

"C'mon Frank. Look at you. You're fallin' apart."

So Frankie takes him by one arm and one of the other guys takes his other arm and they walk him to the private elevator, push the button and send him up. Barbara is waiting for him and puts him to bed. Tears are coming out of Frankie's eyes and running down his face as his heart breaks for his dear friend.

....

While Frankie is hanging out with Sinatra until the "wee small hours of the morning", Frankie's wife, Sue, is at home with the kids. To pass the time, she starts writing songs. She writes a song titled, "*Loving You Too Long To Say Goodbye*". Frankie takes it to Engelbert

Humperdinck's manager at Caesar's Palace and says, "Listen to this song. My wife wrote it and it's really good."

At first, the manager doesn't want to listen to it. But Frankie says, "Don't you remember meeting me with Frank Sinatra last night?" "By George, I do. Yeah, I'll listen to it."

Two weeks later, Humperdinck's manager calls and says, "We love your song and it will be the first song out on Eng's new album, 'This Moment In Time'." It sold 350,000 copies.

....

Frank Rosenphal runs the Stardust for the Chicago Outfit. He's an ego maniac and doesn't like Frankie – probably because Frankie is well-liked and gets a lot of attention. The Chicago Mob guys are in town and they're all sitting around a table at a restaurant in the hotel. Word has gotten around that Rosenphal is closing the Lounge and firing Frankie. The Spilotro brothers, Tony and Michael, are there and Michael says to one of his underlings, "Get Rosenphal in here." Rosenphal comes in and Michael Spilotro says, "We hear you're gonna close down the Lounge."

"Yes sir, that's what I'm planning to do."

"What are ya gonna do with Frankie?"

"Well, Frankie's gotta go. I got no place for him."

"No fuckin' way. Are you crazy? Frankie's not goin' anywhere."

Rosenphal gets all red in the face and starts stuttering, "Wwwell, what am I gonna do with him?"

"Find another job for him. Let him take over somethin' else. Put him wherever he wants'ta go. Frankie's over in the Lounge now. Call him in here."

Spilotro's guy gets up, goes into the Lounge and walks over to Frankie.

"Hey Frankie, there's some guys wanna talk to ya."

"Oh, okay sure," says Frankie. And he walks over to the restaurant.

Michael Spilotro says, "Hey Frankie, sit down. Have a drink."

Rosenphal says, "Hi Frankie."

"Hello Lefty." (Everybody calls Rosenphal "Lefty" to his face, but they call him the "Milk Bottle" when he's not around because he's bald, tall and skinny with skin as white as milk.)

Frankie says, "What's goin' on?"

"Well, you know I'm closing the Lounge," Rosenphal says.

"Yeah, I heard that," says Frankie.

Tony Spilotro says, "Where do you wanna go, Frankie?" "Geez, I dunno."

One of the guys says, "Frankie, why don't you take over the Moby Dick? It's a great restaurant."

"Yeah, it is a great place, but I'm not gonna make any money there."

"Don't worry about that. We'll give you a raise. You'll make plenty."

"Okay," Frankie turns to Rosenphal and says, "but look Lefty, I wouldn't mind doin' that job but I don't need you comin' in and tellin' me what to do."

"No no, Frankie, you take that job and I won't even come into the restaurant. I won't ever both you. You hire and fire anybody you want. That'll be your place."

"Okay." says Frankie. "You guys hear what he's Sayin'?"

Everybody says, "Yeah, we hear."

....

A guy by the name of Paul Lorden runs the Hacienda for the Chicago Outfit. The Casino had losses in pilferage of $320,000 the previous month and Paul calls Frankie asking him to come over to work for him. Paul Lorden and Frank Rosenphal are pretty tight and Frankie knows that this is finally Rosenphal's way of getting Frankie out of the Stardust, but he doesn't care because he's pretty much got the run of the place at the Hacienda. He wears many hats: Food & Beverage Director, Maitre d', Host.

He has seven Captains working for him and he tells them, "You know, this job ain't for free, you understand?" They each pay Frankie anywhere from $150 - $200 a night out of their tokes. Paul Lorden is a good man and he and Frankie become friends.

Redd Foxx comes in one night and says to Frankie, "Man, you're everywhere in Las Vegas. Whadya doin' over here at the Hacienda?"

"Hey Redd, good to see ya."

"Listen Frankie, I'm gonna be doin' a show over here every night at 2AM."

"That's a really good idea, Redd. The show will be a big hit."

Frankie knows that at 2AM all the bar people and the pimps come in. As soon as the word gets out, every night Frankie hears, "Is Redd Foxx gonna be performing here tonight?"

Frankie says, "Yeah, he'll be on in about 30 minutes." "Can you get me a table?"

"Well, I've only got a few tables left, ya know?"

The guy says, "Here man, here's a $20 bill, put this in your pocket."

Frankie looks at the money and says, "What's the matter, you short?" Frankie knows that most of these guys are involved in drugs and prostitution so he doesn't mind taking their money. "Ah, don't worry about it, I'll put you somewhere."

"No, no here, take this." And the guy instead gives Frankie a $50 bill. Frankie makes more money with Redd Foxx at the Hacienda than he has with anything else on the Strip.

....

After a few years, Frankie decides that he's had enough of the casino business. He's greeted more than a million people – from Hollywood royalty, famous politicians and sports stars to Kings and Queens of foreign countries. The MGM has had a fire and Petey is out of a job, so the two brothers decide to open a restaurant. They find a high class Mexican Restaurant at Flamingo and Rainbow that has gone out of business. It's a beautiful place and all the furnishings are still intact. Frankie goes to his bank to try to get an SBA Loan. He meets with one of the bank's loan officers.

"Well, Mr. Basilio, there's $220,000 owed on this business and you would need to assume that debt in order to take over the property. And the bank would need collateral, of course."

"What kind'a collateral would you need?" asks Frankie.

"Well, you and your brother would have to put up your houses and we would need $60,000 cash down."

"All right, I'll get back to you," Frankie tells the Banker.

Frankie leaves the bank and goes to see Petey. They both come up with their share - $30,000 each – and they are prepared to put up their houses as collateral. Frankie returns to the bank.

The same loan officer tells Frankie, "Well, I don't know if you're going to qualify for this loan."

Frankie says, "Who's in charge here?" "That would be Mr. Garnet."

"Call him out here, will ya? Lemme talk to him."

In a few minutes, this little guy walks out. He looks at Frankie and says, "Aren't you the boss at the Stardust?"

"Yeah, I used to be there. I'm at the Hacienda now. You look familiar."

"I'm Bob, Bob Garnet, don't you remember me? You comped me all the time at the Stardust."

"Oh yeah Bob, I remember you. I always put you up front and comped your drinks. Whadya doin' here, Bob?"

"I'm the Senior Vice President of the bank. What do you need, Frank?"

"Well Bob, I wanna assume the loan of $220,000 on a restaurant at Flamingo and Rainbow that went out of business so that my brother and I can open up *Chateau Bella*."

Bob looks at his Loan Officer and says, "So what's wrong?"

"Well sir, I'm just trying to make sure that it's a sound investment."

"Just put him in. Give him the loan."

Bob turns to Frankie and says, "I didn't know you wanted to open a restaurant."

"Well Bob, I didn't know who the hell you were. I thought you were just some bum on the street that I used to comp all the time." They both laugh.

....

Frankie is trying to get a Liquor and Gaming License for the restaurant. Every month he goes in front of the Gaming Board for approval and every month for ten months he is turned down for "unspecified reasons". He knows that his background is likely the reason, but he asks the Board why he is being refused the Licenses and he is told only that he can apply again the next month.

The following month, Frankie brings his lawyers with him to the Board Hearing and when he is refused yet again his lawyers can't get an explanation either. Frankie is so distraught that he grabs a Board member by the name of Coors by the neck and throws him against the wall. "Look, I've been applying for a Liquor and Gaming License for my restaurant every month for eleven months and I keep getting turned down with no explanation. You're taking food out of the mouths of my wife and kids. Next month, if I don't get approved, you're gonna have no more worries, I promise you."

The lawyers are yelling, "Frankie, are you crazy? Put the guy down. You can't threaten a Board member." Coors is shaking like a leaf. The Board meeting ends and Coors goes back to Carson City.

The next month, Frankie is at the Board hearing and when they get to *Chateau Bella*, they announce "Approved for Liquor License"; "Approved for Gaming License".

....

After leaving the Board Hearing, Frankie and his lawyers are approached by two F.B.I. agents. The lead Agent introduces himself as Agent Meadows.

"Are you Frank Basilio?"

"Yeah."

"Will you please come with us?"

Frankie's lawyer asks, "Is this an arrest?"

"No no, we just want to interview Frank."

So they all get into the Feds' car and drive to Maryland Parkway to a vacant store. There's a team of guys there.

Frankie says, "I've got nothin' to hide."

They start mentioning names of different people: "Do you know this guy? Do you know this other guy? Do you know that guy? Do you know Joe Basilio?"

Frankie says, "Of course I know him. He's my brother, but don't even mention him because I don't talk to him anymore. I haven't spoken to him in five years. I couldn't care if he lives or dies." Frankie is just saying this to keep them from asking anymore about his brother.

"Do you know Moe Green?"

Frankie starts to laugh and says, "Everybody knows Moe Green. He was the guy in the Godfather that they shot through the eye. That was Moe Green." Everybody laughs.

"All right, all right, that's enough of that bullshit. I meant to say Moe Dallas."

Frankie says, "I know Moe Dallas, too. Look, I'm not Al Capone. I'm just tryin' to earn a living for my family. I'm no tough guy. I'm no wise guy. I just wanna earn a living."

"Yeah yeah we know, you're not a tough guy. Lemme ask you about Tony Spilotro and Michael Spilotro. Do you know them?"

"Of course I know them. They're friends of mine and good customers. They come in the Lounge like thousands of people – like the Attorney General of

Nevada, the Mayor of Las Vegas, all the Hollywood Stars. It's my business to know people and to greet people. That's what I do. What's the crime in that? I really wish you'd let me go home now because I'm very tired and I have nothing else to tell you."

....

Chateau Bella opens up and is very popular with the Hollywood crowd and wise guys from all over the country. Everybody that Frankie knows from his days on the Strip comes in to eat and socialize including cops, lawyers and politicians. But after a while, people begin to complain that the restaurant is too far out from the Strip where they are comped all the time. Frankie and Petey can't afford to comp everybody, but they end up comping too many people and eventually the restaurant closes.

....

Frankie is an old man now looking back on his life. These days, he lives like a regular guy. A lot of the old people in the retirement community where he lives seem like children. He likes them, but to him they're naive and Frankie has never been naive in his life. It's hard for him to relate to these people, but he talks with them to pass the time.

Its thirty years now since Frankie retired after selling his restaurant. He sits on the sofa in his comfortable house, sometimes watching TV or listening to old-time music. He thinks about his wonderful wife, Sue – gone now, but who put up with him for fifty-six years. Sue knew his ways and loved him without conditions. He thinks about his grown children whom he loves. He spends every weekend now with his Grandson. Tommy is nine years old and the light of Frankie's life. He's made an old Grampa stay afloat and want to live. They go drag car racing and watch movies. Frankie doesn't leave his house too much anymore. He cooks a lot at home and makes his "gravy" and all the old Italian dishes that his Mama and Gramma used to make.

Late one night, the doorbell rings. No one comes to the door at night except maybe a security guard to tell you that your garage door is open or that you've left your trash can out. Lots of rules in these retirement communities. Frankie, being Frankie, grabs his gun and goes to the door.

"Who are you and whadya want?"

"Frank Basilio, this is the F.B.I."

Frankie looks out the window and sees two guys dressed in dark suits and holding up F.B.I. badges. Quickly hiding his gun, he opens the door and asks them in.

"What's on your mind, fellas?"

"Frankie, I'm Special Agent Meadows and this is my partner, Agent Wells.

We're here to ask you a few questions about Rico Capello and Bruno Russo."

"Yeah, I knew those guys about 40 years ago. They're both dead now."

"Our intelligence tells us that you took trips to Chicago with these known mobsters and murderers. And, yes, they both died in prison, but they stashed two million dollars in stolen money somewhere. Your name has come up a few times and we thought you might be able to help us."

"Agent Meadows . . . Meadows. That name's familiar."

"You might remember my father, Frankie. His name was Agent Mike Meadows and he interrogated you many years ago over on Maryland Parkway. So I feel like we're friends, Frankie."

A smile slowly begins to spread across Frankie's face. "If you weren't F.B.I., I'd treat you like a son. But look Agent Meadows, Agent Wells, I'm an old man. I'm 84 years old. Time is my enemy. If I knew anything about that two million bucks, you think I'd be livin' here? You guys just don't give up, do ya?"

THE END